MURDER AT MADAME TUSSAUD'S

LEE STRAUSS

la plume
PRESS

GINGER GOLD MYSTERIES

(IN ORDER)

Murder at the Royal Albert Hall

Murder in Belgravia

Murder on Mallowan Court

Murder at the Savoy

Murder at the Circus

Murder at the Boxing Club

Murder in France

Murder at Yuletide

Murder at Madame Tussauds

Murder at St. Paul's Cathedral

NOTE about the spelling of Madame Tussauds. While the apostrophe is no longer used, in 1928, the setting of this novel, Madame Tussaud's was spelled with an apostrophe, and as such, this is the spelling used in content of this book.

Library and Archives Canada Cataloguing in Publication

Title: Murder at Madame Tussaud's / Lee Strauss.

Names: Strauss, Lee (Novelist), author.

Series: Strauss, Lee (Novelist). Ginger Gold mystery ; 23.Description: Series statement: A Ginger Gold mystery ; 23 | "A 1920s cozy historical mystery."

Identifiers: Canadiana (print) 20230180639 | Canadiana (print) 20230180647 | Canadiana (ebook) 20230180647 | ISBN 9781774092620 (hardcover) | ISBN 9781774092613 (softcover) | ISBN 9781774092644 (IngramSpark softcover) | ISBN 9781774092606 (Kindle) | ISBN 9781774092637 (EPUB)

Classification: LCC PS8637.T739 M85 2023 | DDC C813/.6—dc23

*G*inger Reed, known by some as Lady Gold, stepped into the atrium of Madame Tussaud's wax museum, newly reopened to the public three years after the devastating fire of 1925. She looked at the ceiling several storeys above the ground floor. The galleries and balconies made for a good view of the exhibits below. She admired the lavish decor of deep red carpets set off by wallpaper etched with gold detail in the art *décoratif* style and a profusion of gold trimming along the ceiling mouldings and electric light fixtures.

"If Madame Tussaud is represented by the extravagance and flamboyancy of this decor," Ginger said to her American friend Haley Higgins, "then she's a lady I wish I could've met."

"Only seventy years too late," Haley said. "Madame Tussaud had a colourful and difficult life. She was imprisoned as a Royalist during the French Revolution."

Ginger had done her research on the famous woman as well. "Yes, I know! And then she was forced to make death masks of prisoners killed by guillotine, even some of her close friends."

"That's horrible," Haley said. "But no doubt, the experience led her to her fascination to recreate the dead and the famous with wax." She approached the figure of King George V that greeted newcomers and gazed at it with admiration.

"She was a divorcee as well," Ginger added. "A distinction that must've been unbearable in those days. Even in these modern times, it's a social blight for one's marriage to end, particularly for the gentler sex."

Haley snorted. "Of course it's difficult for women. When is life not?"

Ginger simply hummed at her friend's retort. Haley wasn't wrong, but Ginger was grateful for the strides already made in her lifetime regarding the rights of women. One couldn't forget the hard work of the suffragettes. Ginger had been tickled pink the first time she cast a legal vote, though the privilege was still withheld from British women in their twenties.

She linked her arm with Haley. They were alike when it came to values and social issues but couldn't have been more different in looks. As for height and curves, Ginger was average, whereas Haley was tall and slender. Ginger had embraced her British heritage and corresponding accent, while Haley, though of Irish descent, was thoroughly American. Ginger's red hair was styled in a fashionable bob with curled tips that rested on high cheekbones. Haley's long brunette hair, with its naturally wild curls, was tucked up under her neck in a faux bob, stray, rebellious strands framing her wide jaw in ringlets. They both wore loose-hanging day frocks with low waists and hemlines that ended mid-calf, though Ginger's wardrobe had the quality advantage of originating from her Regent Street dress shop.

"Let's visit the Hollywood exhibit," Ginger suggested. "If anyone has defied societal norms, it's the women in cinema."

"So true," Haley agreed. "Those gals have pluck."

Wandering through the exhibit, face to face with the extremely lifelike wax figures, Ginger felt as if they were actually mingling with the likes of "It Girls" Louise Brooks and Clara Bow; the Hollywood couple called American royalty, Douglas Fairbanks and Mary Pickford; Charlie Chaplin, and Rudolf Valentino.

"You couldn't find two famous actors more different from each other," Ginger said, looking at the curly hair of Mr. Chaplin and the sleek black head of Mr. Valentino.

"It's amazing how closely the wax figures resemble reality," Haley said with sincere appreciation. "My hat's off to the artists."

Ginger agreed. "Nothing tantalises the imagination of the general populace more than gossip about the famous and infamous. And to actually see one's idol—villain or otherwise—the experience is even more delicious. Perhaps one might be fortunate enough to spot a famous person milling about a city such as London, but those who've passed on are impossible to meet."

"Mrs. Reed?"

Ginger turned to the sound of a female voice, her eyes widening in recognition. "Miss Forbes!"

With her flyaway hair and thick brows, Helen Forbes hadn't adopted common beauty trends. She was more of an acquaintance than a friend and was someone with whom Ginger had occasionally crossed paths. Miss Forbes' modern views and outgoing personality appealed to Ginger, and she was always pleased to see her.

"How nice to run into you again," Ginger continued. Turning to Haley, she added, "May I introduce my good friend Miss Haley Higgins from Boston. Haley, this is Miss Helen Forbes. I'm certain the two of you will get on swimmingly. Miss Higgins is in London to continue her studies in medicine. Miss Forbes is a solicitor. You're both rarities in your fields, being female."

"Indeed," Miss Forbes said as she shook Haley's hand. "It's a pleasure to meet you."

"Mine as well," Haley returned.

Miss Forbes waved a gloved hand. "I can't decide if my fascination is morbid or benign."

"What do you mean?" Ginger asked.

With a nod to the collection of actors and actresses, Miss Forbes said, "The way we adore persons simply for pretending to be someone they're not. Oh." Miss Forbes' eyes lit up. "Have you been to the mass murderer exhibit?" She raised a brow. "I confess to being intrigued and feel guilty about it. Particularly since the victims of these horrible people are usually women or children." Catching

Haley's gaze, she continued. "What is your speciality?"

"Pathology," Haley answered.

Miss Forbes laughed. "Then you might quite like that exhibit, though the Dracula one is closer. You'll probably enjoy that one as well."

"Did you?" Ginger asked.

"Oh, yes," Miss Forbes said. "I'm a fan of Bram Stoker's work. Anyway, it was delightful to run into you, Mrs. Reed. A pleasure, Miss Higgins."

Ginger and Haley watched as Miss Forbes walked away with confident strides.

"She's a woman on a mission," Haley said.

"Indeed. Like you, she's had to fight tooth and nail to get where she is, and even though she's done as well in her exams as any man, she's still treated like the receptionists who are rotated out every time one gets married."

Haley's lips pulled up on one side. "I like her."

"She did her bit with the suffragettes, and now she's a voice for all women," Ginger said. "I admire her greatly."

Miss Forbes had been correct when she said the Bram Stoker exhibit came next. Entering the room was like stepping into the mouth of Dracula himself, all bloody reds and small electric lights strung like dripping saliva. The wax figurine depicting the tantalising protagonist was certainly lifelike, at least Ginger thought so, with eyes that were just yellow enough to be otherworldly. The skin was pale with a believable sequence of bluish veins travelling just underneath. He wore a shiny black suit with long tails, a crisp white shirt, and a black bow tie. Thick black hair, gleaming with oil, was combed straight back from a high forehead, perfect for displaying a pointy widow's peak.

The mood was darker than the Hollywood exhibit, with props draped in fake spider's webs and dim lighting. Haley frowned as she considered the fictional icon. "They made him too attractive."

Ginger placed a gloved finger on her chin as she weighed her opinion. "Perhaps a tad. Count Dracula possessed charm and charisma, and indeed, a certain amount of attractiveness, all assets used to deceive his victims."

Few people wandered in and out of the room. Perhaps because the subject was rather macabre, those who enjoyed such things were people who tended to carouse through the evening hours and sleep later through the morning ones. Ginger and Haley were the exceptions.

"Felicia will be disappointed," Ginger said, referring to her late husband's sister. "She so wanted to join us, but alas, the opening date conflicted with her trip to Scotland with Charles."

"The museum will still be here when she gets back," Haley said.

"That's true," Ginger said. "I shan't mind a return visit, should she be in need of company."

"I've noticed the earl is a busy man," Haley said. "I can't think as to what a *lord* does with his time."

Haley didn't share the British appreciation for the class system. But Ginger agreed that she did have a point. Felicia's husband did keep exceedingly busy. At least this time, he had invited his wife to join him on his journey.

"I suppose I shouldn't be surprised to find well-read ladies like yourselves here."

Ginger and Haley turned to the warm male voice and sang his name in unison, "Dr. Palmer!"

The young pathologist was as tall as Haley. He wore a suit with cuffed trousers, his dark hair oiled with a sharp side part, and fashionable two-tone oxford sports shoes.

"Hello, ladies," the doctor returned with a strained but charming smile.

"It's rather a social scene here at Madame Tussaud's," Ginger said.

"You've run into others of your acquaintance, I take it," Dr. Palmer replied, but his eyes had settled on Haley.

"The museum is of great public interest," Haley said. "Are you a fan of Bram Stoker?"

Dr. Palmer shrugged. "Mildly. I found the mass murderer exhibit intriguing." Nodding to Haley he said, "We see all kinds in our line of work, and I'm captivated by the psychology of the murderous mind." He smiled at Ginger. "It might be rather gruesome for a lady like yourself, Mrs. Reed. No need to put grotesque images into your lovely head."

Ginger lifted her chin. "You are aware of my line of work, Doctor?"

"Of course, you assist your husband on occasion." He casually slipped his hands into his trouser pockets. "I suppose you've encountered a degree of unpleasantness."

"It's quite obvious you're new to London," Haley said lightly. "Mrs. Reed is well known in these parts for her private detective work."

Dr. Palmer had the grace to look sheepish. "How frightfully dense of me. Of course I'm aware of your reputation."

"And you must remember we've recently worked together," Ginger added.

"Indeed," Dr. Palmer conceded. "It was a joy. I hope you'll forgive my thoughtlessness, Mrs. Reed. I've had plenty going on of late to clutter my mind."

"There's no need to apologise," Ginger said with a smile.

Dr. Palmer turned his attention back to Haley. "I'll see you later at the mortuary, won't I?"

Haley nodded. "It's on my calendar for the day."

"Very good. Ta-ta, ladies." Dr. Palmer pivoted and strolled out, leaving Ginger and Haley in his wake.

"He's rather intense, isn't he?" Ginger said.

"He loves his work."

Ginger caught the note of defensiveness in Haley's voice. "You fancy him, don't you?"

Haley scoffed. "I don't *fancy* him. I admire him. That's different. I want him to teach me, not court me."

Ginger turned back to the handsome Dracula figure, hiding her smile from Haley, who, Ginger surmised, most definitely fancied the good doctor.

Haley, firmly closing the door on the subject, turned her attention to Dracula's current victim. A young lady's form was sprawled out on a plush red velvet settee, a thin arm hung over the edge. Painted fingernails brushed the ornate wooden settee leg where it met the red carpet. The blond wig was pinned atop the figure's head in Victorian fashion. In keeping with the theme, two red dots had been painted on her neck, the work of the handsome vampire.

"I'm surprised at the detail inaccuracy of the artist," Haley said. "Teeth marks of a grown man, vampire or not, would be further apart by at least twice." She frowned as she studied the figure, lines forming on her wide forehead.

Ginger stepped closer. "Is something the matter?"

"Do you smell that?" Haley asked.

Ginger sniffed, then scrunched up her nose. "A faint rancidity. A dead rat nearby?"

Rats were practically synonymous with London, and even though the museum was newly built, it wasn't possible to construct a structure impervious to vermin.

On closer look, Ginger noted a difference in the wax quality used on this figure compared with the others. "It's rather shoddily created," she said. "Perhaps the artists ran out of the premium wax."

Haley ran a fingernail along the arm, carving a line, and Ginger nearly scolded her for touching the exhibit, but then she saw the discrepancy.

"Oh mercy," Ginger said. "Is that real skin?"

Haley ran a finger along the figure's arm, leaving an indentation, then grimaced as she held Ginger's gaze. "I believe this to be a bona fide corpse, Ginger."

Ginger pursed her lips. "A bona fide murder, you mean?"

2

*G*inger, hearing feet shuffling and the muttering of voices, glanced over her shoulder in time to see a small group crossing the threshold into the room. She lifted a gloved hand. "I'm afraid this exhibit is closed."

A man in a long overcoat frowned, and his bushy eyebrows furrowed. "And what authority do you have to close the exhibit?"

"I'm Mrs. Reed, the wife of a chief inspector, and this is Miss Higgins, a nurse and student of pathology. And you are, sir?"

"Harris. I'm with my family, and we most especially wanted to visit the Bram Stoker exhibit."

Ginger tried a softer approach. "Sir, my colleague

and I believe a crime has been committed, and as such, it would be unfitting for your family to enter. Would you be so good as to summon the museum manager? I believe his name is Mr. Arthur Keene."

Mr. Harris craned his neck to see what Ginger and Haley were trying to conceal with the careful positioning of their bodies. She forced the man to hold her gaze. "And please ring Scotland Yard. My husband, Chief Inspector Reed, in particular."

The man seemed to reconsider. Instead of forcing his way in with his family, he instructed his wife and two sons to wait in the corridor. "I'll return shortly," he said before darting out. "If this is a practical joke, I'll have you know that I'm a solicitor."

"We are deadly serious, sir," Haley stated.

When the man and his family had stepped out of the room, Ginger quickly positioned the two bronze posts with the burgundy velvet rope hanging between them in front of the entrance and turned off most lights, hoping it would prevent others from entering.

"I wonder if Dr. Palmer is still on site," Haley said.

"Go and see if you can find him," Ginger replied. "I'll wait here with the body to ensure nothing is disturbed."

Haley cast her a look as if she was about to ask Ginger if she was sure she wanted to stay alone in the room with a corpse but then thought better of it.

Ginger wasn't as used to being in the presence of the deceased as Haley, but she'd seen her share of corpses, both whilst acting as a private detective in London, and before that, during the long war years. Still, it wasn't something she wanted to get used to.

Being alone in the exhibit, especially in its dimmed state, was rather unnerving, but it also allowed Ginger to examine the victim. She rummaged through her handbag—she kept sundry unusual tools there, including a set of lock picks, a magnifying glass, a torch, and a palm-sized Remington pistol. Retrieving her torch and magnifying glass, she went to work.

The victim was a young woman. A slender physique under the mountain of fabric needed for a typical nineteenth-century frock. Ginger pressed her fingers against the torso, its bony firmness confirming a corset. Dr. Palmer and Haley would thoroughly examine the body at the mortuary, so Ginger focused her beam on the woman's long, slender neck and the two red dots there. About half an inch apart, the punctures themselves didn't seem like something that could bring on death. Perhaps if one of them had pierced the jugular, but then there would be profuse bleeding to contend with.

No, Ginger suspected some manner of poison had been administered through the neck.

Mr. Harris returned with the manager, Mr. Keene. "That will do," Mr. Keene said, stopping Mr. Harris. Moving the barrier so he alone could slip through, he added, "I can take care of this now. I'm much obliged to you for summoning me quickly."

Dismissed, Mr. Harris left with a grunt of dissatisfaction. Mr. Keene had a wide nose and dark, deep-set eyes. He narrowed his gaze at Ginger. "I understand you took closing this exhibit upon yourself."

"I'm afraid it was necessary," Ginger returned. She waved a hand to the body on the settee. "You've got a crime on your hands."

Mr. Keene bent his long, slender body, arching over the victim as if he feared getting too close. "Blast it! This is very bad for business, very bad indeed." Standing tall, he held the back of his neck. "I can confirm that the figure lying here yesterday was made completely of wax."

"Do you have any idea where one might swiftly dispose of such a thing?" Ginger asked.

Mr. Keene's eyes moved to a decorative wardrobe

in the room. "Perhaps there?" With long strides, he moved to the wardrobe and pulled on the door, which seemed locked, with no key in sight.

"Deuced door!"

"Allow me," Ginger said, her lock picks already in her gloved hand.

"What on earth ... ?"

Ginger got to work on the lock with two pins. "I shall allow that a lady possessing a set of lock picks is an oddity. But I assure you, it's quite legitimate."

"I can hardly imagine how—" Mr. Keene went silent as the lock pins clicked and the door swung open. Inside, the mangled wax figure was stuffed into a space much too small, its dress and corset missing. Mr. Keene continued, "It seems we've solved one mystery."

"And what mystery is that?"

Ginger turned to Haley's voice. Dr. Palmer was with her and stepped around the barrier.

"The mystery of where the original wax figurine had been deposited," Ginger said, motioning to the corpse. "Dr. Palmer, you must be extremely curious."

"Indeed," Dr. Palmer said as he stepped to the victim's side. "Might we brighten the lighting?"

Haley reached for the switch and turned on the

overhead lights, nearly blinding everyone temporarily with the sudden brightness. "We turned them down to keep the museum clientele from wandering in," she explained.

"How long do you think she's been dead?" Ginger asked.

Dr. Palmer lifted his chin in Haley's direction. "What do you think, Miss Higgins?"

Haley's brow furrowed as she did a cursory examination. "She's chilled, though the museum is kept cooler because of the wax." Haley lifted the corpse's arm. "Rigor has come and gone. You can see in the exposed skin of her shoulders that lividity has occurred."

Ginger noted a defining line where the blood had settled along the lower side of the body. "She's been in a lying position for some time."

"I'd say a good eight to ten hours," Haley said. "Dr. Palmer?"

Dr. Palmer offered a quick nod. "I would concur." He bent low to study the neck marks. "I've seen many oddities in my line of work, but this one is brilliantly absurd."

At Mr. Keene's look of consternation, Ginger made belated introductions. "This is Dr. Palmer. He's a pathologist at the University College Hospital. With him is Miss Haley Higgins, who is an intern with Dr. Palmer. Mr. Keene is the general manager of the museum."

Mr. Keene raised narrow, dark brows, his eyes set on Haley. "An intern?"

"Yes, Mr. Keene," Haley answered. "In this modern age, opportunities for women are opening up in many fields dominated by men."

Haley had no qualms when it came to staking her ground. She was the same height as Mr. Keene, and he backed down under her piercing gaze. Ginger felt now was an opportune time to intervene before words were spoken out of turn. "Mr. Keene, perhaps you wouldn't mind guarding the door. All museum guests must be kept out. The police should be here shortly."

Ginger glanced at the dainty wristwatch on her narrow wrist and wondered what was keeping Basil. She didn't have to wait long; soon, she could hear his voice filling the outer corridor. "Just direct me to the Dracula exhibit, my good fellow. I've no interest in a tour at the moment."

Basil's form filled the doorway to the exhibit. Though not a domineering man, Basil had a natural, unassuming essence of authority, enhanced by his fine suit and the carefully knotted tie at his neck. Lines had formed around lovely hazel eyes, and his temples had grown greyer with time. Many people cowered at his presence when they learned of his rank at Scotland Yard, but Ginger's knees weakened at the sight of her handsome husband. She approached him, and he asked gently, "Did you discover the body?"

"No, Haley noticed the discrepancy at first," Ginger answered.

Haley chimed in. "I noticed the smell first. It's slight, but I have a well-working nose."

As if on cue, everyone took a sniff.

"The body is still blanching," Haley continued. She pressed the forearm of the corpse, and two white spots appeared. "Blanching occurs eight to ten hours after death, and then the blood becomes too fixed for any further changes in colour to occur. She was deposited here during the night."

Basil stepped to the body and frowned as he stared at the dots on the neck. Not a simple frown in Ginger's mind, as one would do when viewing something unpleasant, but a frown verging on a scowl. Basil's jaw tightened, his lip twitched involuntarily, and his shoulders stiffened.

Ginger ducked to catch her husband's eyes. She knew him well enough to know when something was wrong, and instinctively she knew what was bothering him now.

"Basil," she began, "this isn't the first time you've seen this modus operandi, is it?"

3

*B*asil Reed had been a member of the Metropolitan Police since 1919. He'd been invalided from the war in its first year and sent home from France with a missing spleen, his tail between his legs. His well-connected parents were influential and rescued his reputation by pulling strings and getting him a position at Scotland Yard so he could "do his bit" for the war effort, chin held high.

Only, they hadn't anticipated their son wanting to stay on the force when the war ended. It certainly didn't pay well, and police work was for the commoner. They considered his refusal to step away a "grievous insolence". But Basil found it gave him reason to get up in the morning, and in those days, when his first wife was estranged and wayward, he'd needed a reason.

And he'd found personal satisfaction in the work. It turned out he was good at it and, over time, had solved many complicated cases, which led to rapid promotions and ultimately to his advancement to chief inspector.

However, not every case was solved, and Basil's chest tightened when he thought of the file of cold cases. He tensed at the notion that people walked about, willy-nilly, getting away with murder.

Or murders.

Ginger was correct in her deduction that he'd seen this method of death before. This woman, positioned on the settee in the Dracula exhibition in Madame Tussaud's wax museum, was in fact, the fourth victim with such marks on her neck. Not since Jack the Ripper had London seen a mass murderer like this. At least this killer wasn't as savage in his methods, but the women were dead, just the same. And who was to say that Jack, who might still be alive, hadn't decided to change his modus operandi?

"Basil?"

Basil turned his attention back to his wife. "This woman is not the first, I'm afraid. There are three others."

Ginger cocked her head as she considered him. She was much too beautiful for this line of work. Her eyes were too green, with that delightful twinkle, and her lips too full and red. Her hair, a lovely copper-red, was too easy to spot in a crowd if one had nefarious notions.

He let out a soft sigh. He'd known what he was getting into when he married her. Her natural beauty only touched the surface of what constituted innate grace and a brilliant, intelligent mind. Ginger's casual, light-hearted manner cloaked a side of her that was daring, mysterious, and Basil had to admit, rather frightening.

"You never mentioned the deaths," she said, her gaze locked on his. "And there's been no mention of them in the newspapers or on the wireless."

"It was decided that news of the killings might needlessly alarm the citizens of London."

Haley scoffed, and Basil jerked. For a moment, he'd forgotten that he and Ginger weren't alone in the room.

"My guess," Haley began as she pushed flyaway curls off her face, "is that these women were from a societal class deemed unworthy of the news. Otherwise, genteel ladies would be locked up on their estates for safekeeping."

Basil sheepishly glanced at his shoes. Haley wasn't wrong. The dead women with neck markings had all been "women of the night".

Palmer cleared his throat. "No bodies with such markings have come through my mortuary."

"Dr. Gupta saw the first one," Basil said, "so naturally, the rest also went to him."

Ginger waved at the corpse on the settee, flicking her fingers at the room. "Have the other victims also been discovered in a unique situation?"

Basil shook his head. "No. They've been found on the streets, in gutters, and in various degrees of decomposition." He nodded at Dracula's victim. "This is new."

Palmer tugged on his trouser legs and then squatted for a better view of the victim's neck. Haley hovered nearby. "Dr. Palmer?" Basil asked. "What do you make of this?"

"It's unlikely she perished because of that puncture wound." The doctor straightened as he continued, "The jugular vein doesn't appear to have been damaged, if it had, she would've bled profusely."

"Poison, then?" Haley said.

Palmer shrugged a shoulder. "That would be my guess, but an autopsy would give a definitive answer."

"Such a bizarre fashion to administer it," Ginger said. "Though whoever is responsible for this wanted it to look like a scene from Dracula. But that doesn't explain the other women."

Basil had been thinking the same thing. "Perhaps the killer was hoping for some notoriety, but the museum kept delaying the opening by days, upsetting the killer's strategic plan of events.

"Is it possible that the other three women were slated for this display, but when the museum failed to open as planned, they were unceremoniously dispatched to the streets?" Ginger asked.

Haley worked her lips. "That makes sense to me."

"Perhaps this exhibit should be closed until the case is solved," Ginger said, her gaze returning to Basil. "It could prevent another tragedy."

"I can get the Yard to keep it closed for a while," Basil said, "but Mr. Keene is sure to make a fuss. This exhibit is a tremendous draw."

Braxton arrived with two ambulance attendants in tow. "The ambulance is in the alley at the back, off

York Terrace West," he announced. "I've got officers stationed to hold back the nosy parkers."

"Very good," Basil said. Then, with a chin nod to Palmer, he asked, "Would you like to do this one? A fresh set of eyes and all that?"

Palmer nodded back. "If you don't think Gupta will mind."

"He's got his hands full with a bout of whooping cough," Basil said. "My bet is he'd be grateful."

Palmer left with the body, and Haley went with them, leaving Basil alone in the room with Ginger. He could hear Braxton speaking to Keene, who wasn't happy that the exhibit was being closed, but Braxton handled the irate manager with professional diplomacy. Keene huffed but accepted his loss, turning on his heel and storming away. The constable peeked in, and Basil gave him a look indicating that he should watch at the door until he himself had finished a final perusal of the scene.

Basil jotted notes in his notebook, the stub of his pencil smudging its thick lines. He was aware of Ginger lingering, astutely taking everything in.

"I'm rather surprised you never thought to mention these poor women to me," she said.

Basil inhaled, moving his gaze away from his

wife, sightlessly scanning the space above her head. The truth was, he was frightened for Ginger. Despite her record of competence and intuitiveness when solving complex cases, Basil felt a growing need to protect her from London's dark underbelly. When they met, she had been a childless widow. Now they had two children to consider, and the thought of losing Ginger was more than Basil could bear. It was bad enough that she worked as a private investigator, and Basil could only reassure himself, knowing that most of her cases were benign.

But this, this madman, was different.

Basil tensed to keep from shivering as his mind went to the letter he'd received just before the first killing was discovered. The writer had used red ink, much like Jack the Ripper had in his infamous letters, and that was when Basil thought that perhaps "Jack" had returned. But the "vampire killer", as this writer called himself, wrote shorter notes, and so far, his murders were far less gruesome. He had penned a note to Basil specifically. It read:

Chief Inspector,

You don't know "jack". Perhaps I am he? I'll not say that I am or not, only to keep you on your toes. What we

have in common, should we not be the same, is that one
kill is not enough. It's never enough.

    D

"Basil?" Ginger prompted, bringing Basil's mind back to the present.

"I didn't want to bother you with a gruesome case like this. You're busy enough with your shop and running Hartigan House. Besides, Morris would disapprove of my discussing every case with my wife."

Ginger huffed. "Since when have you cared what Superintendent Morris thought?"

Basil pursed his lips. Ginger wasn't wrong. Morris was an oaf who'd got his position because of *who* he knew rather than *what* he knew. "I don't care, so to speak, but he's still my superior."

"Are you afraid he'll demote you for insolence?" Ginger said, her thin, arched brows rising higher. "I hardly think he'd dare, with your track record. Besides, he's suffered your indignation and hasn't done more than bluster and bluff."

"A man can be pushed too far, love."

Ginger's features softened as she smiled. She took his hand and whispered, "I'm not pushing you too far, am I?"

If they weren't in a public place, with Braxton

only feet away, Basil would've grabbed her in a firm embrace and kissed her. She did not know how she affected him, how a simple smile and show of affection caused him to buzz with electricity.

He squeezed her hand before letting it go and stepping back.

4

*W*ith the Dracula exhibit closing, the victim being examined in the mortuary by Haley and Dr. Palmer, and Basil returning with Braxton to Scotland Yard, Ginger headed back to Hartigan House. Driving her 1924 pearly-white Crossley, Ginger gripped the polished-wood steering wheel as she manoeuvred around the horses and carts, the lumbering double-decker motor buses, and a smattering of pedestrians who seemed to care more for their hats than their very lives. Ginger slammed on the brakes as a distracted walker dodged in front of her. Pinching the black ball of her brass horn in protest gave Ginger a thrill, and she understood why so many seemed delighted to honk their horns at her.

The journey from Madame Tussaud's museum on Marylebone Road to Hartigan House in South Kensington took her through the familiar settings of Hyde Park and Kensington Gardens. It gave her plenty of time to ponder the extraordinary events of the morning. What had begun as an enjoyable outing with Haley had turned into a macabre crime scene.

As troubling as it was to discover the poor woman's dead body, Ginger found Basil's reticence to share such an intriguing case with her even more so. She understood Basil couldn't share everything about his work with her, just as she had certain confidences to keep with her work at Lady Gold Investigations. Still, his silence probably had nothing to do with confidentiality commitments.

Pushing that aside, Ginger turned to the cause of death. Haley's guess at poison was most likely correct unless other abuses were discovered underneath the costume. What needed to be established now was what kind of poison. Had it been administered through the puncture wound? Or had it been delivered another way, and the neck marks were simply a distraction?

Ginger had become so consumed with the murder that she didn't notice a vegetable wagon pull out in front of her until a second too late. Quick reflexes had her tugging on the steering wheel as she slammed on the brakes. Unbelievably, the driver in question had the gall to shake his fist at her! Ginger snorted, putting the Crossley in reverse and barely touching the lorry parked behind her, she pulled back into the mass of London traffic.

Soon she was motoring down the lane behind Mallowan Court and turning into the drive behind Hartigan House. Ginger had inherited the limestone structure and the oversized property when her father passed away. At first, she'd planned to sell her childhood home and return to Boston, but then she'd met Basil and her adopted son, Scout, and as they said, the rest was history.

After parking the Crossley in front of the garage, she handed the keys to her gardener. "Thank you, Clement."

Clement enjoyed driving her motorcar, and even the simple act of moving it into the garage seemed to give him joy.

"My pleasure, madam." Clement pulled up on one trouser leg of his overall and slid onto the soft red upholstery before casting an appreciative glance back at Ginger. He then guided the machine into its spot. The space beside it was reserved for Basil's green Austin 7, which Ginger could picture sitting in the car park near Victoria Embankment. Helping Clement with garden and garage oversight was Marvin Elliot, Scout's older cousin, who was leading a horse out of the stable at that moment. Marvin had had a rough go through life, and an accident had given him a brain injury. To prevent the lad from living dangerously on the street, Ginger had opened her home—and heart—to him, giving him a job and a room in the attic.

Marvin touched the peak of his flat cap. "G'day, madam."

"Hello, Marvin." She approached her majestic golden-haired Akhal-Teke and stroked its long nose. "How is Goldmine today?"

"Very well, madam. Just off to stretch the legs, then I'll give Sir Blackwell 'is turn."

Sir Blackwell, a lovely Arabian, came to Hartigan House with Basil. Ginger and Basil often rode their horses through Kensington Gardens and Hyde Park. Once this confounded case was behind them, she'd ensure they went for a long ride.

"Thank you for taking such good care of them," Ginger said. "Scout is relieved to know you're here in his absence." The horses particularly interested Scout, who went to a boarding school specially designed for equine enthusiasts, and when he was home, the fifteen-year-old spent a great deal of time in the stable.

"It's 'ardly work for me, madam." Marvin grinned. "I could sleep in the stables and not mind a bit."

Ginger smiled back. "I think you'd get a better rest in your room."

Thanks to Clement being green-fingered, the back garden was awakened for spring loveliness. Ambrosia, the dowager Lady Gold and Ginger's former grandmother-in-law, liked to claim credit for its ongoing beauty, though most of her contributions of late had been from her position on a patio chair, dictating orders. Ginger had to credit Clement's patience with the elderly matriarch. He knew the dowager better than most, having been in her service for years before his time at Hartigan House. Ambrosia and Felicia, Ambrosia's granddaughter and Ginger's former sister-in-law, had moved in with Ginger along with Clement and a couple of other servants in tow, after their home had burned down.

Ginger stepped into the rear entrance of Hartigan House, only making it a few steps before being approached by Pippins, her elderly butler. The shoulders of his tall and slender form had folded over with time, his head became shiny and bald, his skin loose on sharp cheekbones. The skin around his cornflower-blue eyes was soft and wrinkled, but the twinkle in them that Ginger remembered from her childhood remained. He held out his arm and accepted her woven, fur-trimmed coat.

Ginger smoothed out the front of her day frock, a delightful new chiffon in jade green. The bodice had vertical lines to match an asymmetric neckline, the skirt a sunburst of plaiting. The fashions in the previous year had hinted at shorter hemlines and narrower seam lines, but the spring line of 1928 made no reservations. The belt line of her new spring and summer wardrobe would be higher by a good inch or three, and Ginger did not doubt that a cinched waistline would return at some point.

She asked Pippins, "Where's Digby?"

She'd employed Digby to take over Pippins' role in the hope her elderly butler would retire, especially after a recent injury, and spend the rest of his days in leisure. However, as Pippins' recovery progressed, the less interested he was in "puttering about", and Ginger didn't have the heart to strip him of his official title, so Digby, between Pippins and Ginger, was now called the "under butler". Ginger was careful not to use the term around Digby, who would most certainly and rightfully consider the demotion an insult, and she didn't want him to leave her staff.

"Digby can't be everywhere at once, madam."

Ginger fought back a grin. She was quite certain Pippins had mastered that feat throughout the years.

"I'm sure he is duly occupied," she said.

"He's assessing the wine cellar. I'll hang your coat up in the cloakroom, madam."

"Thank you, Pips." She almost admonished him to take it easy for the rest of the day but bit her tongue in time. Her beloved butler had his pride.

Ginger walked quickly, her white patent leather two-strap pumps clicking along the black-and-white marble-tiled floor. Beyond the green baize door, she could hear the bustling in the kitchen as Mrs. Beasley commanded the efforts of her helpers as they prepared for the remaining meals of the day.

The corridor led to the vast entrance hall. A large wooden door was flanked by tall windows facing Mallowan Court. A staircase adorned with a plush emerald-green runner curled up to the upper floor where the bedrooms, the library, and baby Rosa's nursery were found. One could look down on the entrance from the railing along the upper corridor. A massive electric chandelier hung from the tall ceiling, brightening the space with glimmering lights. A drawing room was right off the entrance hall, opposite the sitting room on the left. The door to the drawing room was cracked open, and Ginger heard the mumbled sounds of female voices. She recognised one as belonging to Ambrosia, the dowager Lady Gold and her former grandmother through marriage.

The dowager's social calendar had decreased as she aged, and gloomy weather kept her either in the sitting room or library over a cup of tea and with her maid Langley reading aloud, now that her eyes had got too bad for her to read herself. Who could she be entertaining?

Activity at the top of the staircase caught Ginger's attention, and she smiled at the sight of Rosa bundled up in Nanny Green's arms.

"Oh, Mrs. Reed," the nanny said as she descended. "You're back. I was just going to take the little miss out in the pram. Get out of the nursery for a while."

"A terrific idea," Ginger said as she held her arms out. Nanny Green deposited little Rosa into Ginger's arms, and she gave her small daughter a snuggle. "How is my Rosa?"

Rosa smiled, her round red cheeks glowing as

she said, "Mama." She reached for Ginger's dangling earrings with a chubby palm, Ginger cupping it in time. "They're very pretty, aren't they?" she asked. "But not for touching."

"How was Madame Tussaud's wax museum, madam?" Nanny Green asked as Ginger handed Rosa back to her. "Is it all they say it is?"

"It's rather impressive," Ginger said. Her mind immediately went to the poor woman found dead there. "But not all the exhibits are open."

"Is that so?" Nanny Green said. "I intend to go on my next day off. I hope they have everything in order by then." She and Rosa disappeared down the corridor to the back garden where the pram was stored.

Instead of heading up the staircase, Ginger moved to the drawing room, tapping lightly on the door before stepping inside. Where the sitting room would be called cosy and comfortable, the drawing room had an air of sophistication, aided by the presence of a baby grand piano in the corner. A fire had been lit in the stone fireplace—as the spring temperatures weren't enough to fend off the chill—and the decor had softer greens, roses, and yellows in the fabrics and wall coverings.

Interestingly, the guest Ginger found sharing tea

with Ambrosia was Mrs. Schofield, their widowed neighbour and not one of Ambrosia's favourite people. The two silver-haired ladies were so animatedly engaged that neither noticed Ginger.

"In our day, a lady of ill repute was easily recognisable," Ambrosia blustered. The soft folds of her cheeks were pink with emotion. "By how they dressed and styled their hair." As if to emphasise her words, she moved a veined hand with bent and bejewelled fingers along her house frock and the grey hair tied and pinned up at the back of her neck.

Mrs. Schofield nodded her more-white-than-grey head in her agreement. "It's no longer easy to say that a woman walking the streets wearing make-up is a tart. They sell make-up at Selfridges now, for anyone to buy!"

Oh mercy. Ginger had expected dull conversation on spring gardening or the aches and pains of ageing. She announced her presence by chirping, "Good day, ladies."

Ambrosia startled, stared over her shoulder, and harrumphed when she saw it was Ginger. "There's no need to sneak up on us, Georgia."

The dowager only used Ginger's Christian name when she was riled up.

"Is everything all right?" Ginger asked, stepping closer.

Mrs. Schofield smiled up at her. "Certainly. We're in the midst of a lively conversation."

"Are you having tea?" Ginger said. "Perhaps I'll join you for a cup." She pulled on the bell rope before sitting in an armchair. "So, what is the topic of the day?"

Ambrosia sipped her tea and then returned the cup to its matching saucer. "Mrs. Schofield and I are rallying ladies to support Gerald Hall in the forthcoming County Council election. He's standing as an independent candidate to become a councillor."

Ginger didn't bother holding in her surprise. "Politics? Since when have you been interested in that?"

Ambrosia was a privileged elite-class member and rarely affected by government policies. When politics had come up in the past, she claimed to be too old for such concerns and preferred to leave those matters to the youth.

"I never have," Ambrosia admitted, "until now. Things are going too far, and I must do my bit to bring correction. For the sake of my grandchild and future great grandchildren."

"I doubt Felicia will stop wearing make-up,

Grandmother." Felicia had prided herself on belonging to the rise of the "Bright Young Things" and had spent many years exasperating her grandmother and Ginger with her bent towards excessive living. This had gone beyond make-up and rising hemlines, freedom from restrictive corsets, and short, boyish hairstyles—all things Ginger herself enjoyed—to wild parties with unabashed drinking, smoking, dancing, and flirting. Often, this had landed her with unflattering photographs and write-ups in the society pages. Her marriage to an earl, Charles Davenport-Witt, had brought on a calming maturity, as had a recent maternal loss. "Surely there are more pressing concerns?" Ginger continued, keeping her attention on Ambrosia. "World hunger or world peace, for instance."

Ambrosia jutted her nose into the air. "The issue is deeper than colour on the lips or rising hemlines. Uncouth behaviour of that sort represents a threat to the national order. It's an offence against social stability."

"That's a direct quote from Mr. Hall," Ginger said. "I heard him declare it over the wireless." Along with other questionable comments. Fascist leanings were taking root in certain circles, and Mr. Hall had made it clear he was chummy with the sort.

Ambrosia huffed. "It doesn't make it less true."

Grace, one of the maids, arrived with a pot of tea. "I heard you had returned, Mrs. Reed. Forgive me for assuming if this wasn't the reason you rang the bell."

Ginger smiled. "It was, in fact, the reason. Thank you." Once Ginger had her tea prepared, and the maid was excused, the conversation returned to the trouble on the streets of London.

"We need a stronger deterrent to get such women away from our menfolk," Mrs. Schofield said.

Ginger's eyebrows jumped. "And you believe arresting them is the answer?"

Ambrosia answered for her neighbour. "Perhaps not the answer, Ginger, but it's a start. We must do something."

"Why not arrest the men who use them?" Ginger offered. "Are they not as equal to the problem as the women?"

Ambrosia and Mrs. Schofield stared back with a look of horror, their eyes bulging and mouths falling open. "Are you quite mad?" Ambrosia finally said. "Since the war, we've had so few young men as it is. We can't very well be locking them up in jail now."

Ginger took a long sip of tea. The morality of prostitution in Britain was of great debate, so much so that a committee had been set up to address it, and a document known as the Macmillan Report was published. In retrospect, Ginger shouldn't have been surprised to find Ambrosia and Mrs. Schofield discussing the issue. She imagined many tea parties across London where the same thing was being deliberated upon: how to eliminate the blight of prostitution.

Unfortunately, someone in London had taken the law into his own hands, the unnamed woman from the Dracula exhibit his fourth victim.

5

*H*aley shared a taxicab to the mortuary with Dr. Palmer, who quickly paid the driver before she could get her change purse from her handbag.

"Allow me," Dr. Palmer said. "It's a hospital expense now."

Fearing he'd do the chivalrous thing and rush around the taxicab to open the door for her, Haley made haste to unlatch it and stepped out onto the kerb, one wide pant leg at a time, before Dr. Palmer reached her. Her feelings for the doctor were muddled. He was kind, well spoken, intelligent, and new to London as she was. However, Haley had every intention of returning to Boston at some point, so a London romance would be a waste of time and emotional energy.

Besides, Dr. Palmer wasn't interested in her that way. He was a natural gentleman to all the women he met.

All the same, Haley made the most of her long strides, keeping a short distance ahead of Dr. Palmer as they strode down the familiar path to the hospital entrance. She intended to reach the door first. However, Dr. Palmer skipped ahead at the last moment, grabbing the handle. Opening it wide, he said, "Ladies first."

Haley obliged. "Thank you."

Feeling a little silly, Haley let out a quiet breath as they headed down the stairs, side by side, and once the mortuary doors were in sight, she asserted her professionalism. "Most certainly, we've arrived before the body," she said.

Dr. Palmer agreed. "That's quite likely. However, there are other matters to tie up before we can focus on the museum victim."

After removing her three-quarter-length spring jacket, Haley found a blank corpse identification form and began to fill it out, printing UNKNOWN in the name section. She was glad that pencil could be erased. Everyone deserved to have their legal name acknowledged.

Glancing across the room, Haley watched Dr. Palmer's profile as he sat at his desk and scribbled away with his favourite fountain pen. The doctor had the telephone receiver at his ear, speaking, quite likely, with the Lord Mayor, who'd asked to be kept informed of this disturbing case. Dr. Palmer nodded as he said, "Yes, sir. A blight on this fair city."

With the paperwork ready, Haley washed her hands in the porcelain sink, using the small mirror as a guide as she pinned strands of curly hair off her face, then donned a long white apron. Her next job was to prepare the surgical table, wash it with soap and water, and let it dry as she prepared a tray of medical instruments.

Sometimes, bodies seemed to stack up in London, even with the hospital mortuaries, but fortunately, this moment wasn't one of them. When the woman's body arrived, they began examining it immediately.

Haley and Dr. Palmer stripped "Unknown" of her wig and costume until the body was as nude as it had been when it came into the world. They gave the deceased the professional courtesy of covering her nakedness with a sheet, exposing the areas of the body in sections as they made their inspection.

"Some bruising on the forearms," Haley said. "Possibly an attempted struggle, but by the time she realised she was in danger, it was too late."

"The neck markings appear to match the other victims," Dr. Palmer said, "but I've only got police photographs to go on."

"Is that what you were studying at your desk?" Haley asked.

When he offered a short nod, Haley couldn't help but feel a little put out that he hadn't offered to show them to her, not that he was obligated to.

He must've sensed her displeasure as he stared at her suddenly, then said, "I put the envelope on the table if you want to look at them."

Mollified, Haley picked up the scalpel and held it out. "Dr. Palmer?"

"You go ahead. I've had plenty of practice making the Y incision."

"The psychology behind these killings intrigues me," Haley said as she completed the last cut.

Dr. Palmer nodded. "Killers kill for many reasons."

"It's one thing to kill another human being—

we're both aware of the myriad of motives—but to put a victim on display as this one was."

"A level of creative madness."

"Exactly," Haley said. "Even to present a poisoning with these marks on the neck, when a simple injection or addition to a person's meal would do."

"Perhaps he or she is trying to make a statement."

Haley liked to be open-minded about the sex of a killer, and women did tend towards poisoning as their choice of weapon. But placing the body at the museum suggested someone with more physical might.

"I would be interested in conversing with Dr. Gupta regarding the other victims," Haley said.

"Oh." Dr. Palmer inclined his head. "Do you know Dr. Gupta personally?"

"I studied under him at the London Medical School for Women."

"I'm told he's a rather handsome man," Dr. Palmer said.

Haley laughed. "He is, but fortunately for his patients, they are already without a pulse. And he has a beautiful bride and family."

"Ah." Dr. Palmer's gaze moved from the bloody

cavity in the corpse's chest, catching Haley's eyes. "Then I don't have to worry about competition."

Haley's jaw dropped. "I don't understand. Competition for what?"

"For your attention, Miss Higgins. Surely you must know that I'm interested in you." Dr. Palmer's lips turned down. "Unless I'm misreading the signs?"

What signs? What signs! Haley blinked. "I'm not sure it's wise for an intern to become overly friendly with the doctor she's being mentored by."

"Those are outdated concepts, are they not?" Dr. Palmer pressed. "I gathered you to be modern and forward-thinking."

Haley *was* modern and forward-thinking. It didn't make her point less valid though.

Dr. Palmer smiled. "Just dinner, to get to know one another better. Surely no harm can come from that. You do eat, don't you?"

Haley swallowed hard. Wasn't this the very thing she'd dreamed of? She couldn't deny her attraction to the pathologist, but the fact that he felt the same way about her left her breathless. Haley felt she had a sober evaluation of her own looks and presentation. She wasn't hideous to look at, but the word "plain" wouldn't be out of place. Her height and slender build didn't exactly ooze femininity, and in trousers, she could be mistaken for a young man, at least from a distance.

But she'd been told she had lovely eyes and a pleasing smile. And if a man found intelligence appealing in a woman—and from Haley's experience, many men did not—well, there was no reason not to believe that Dr. Palmer's interest in her was genuine.

"Miss Higgins?" Dr. Palmer said, pulling her from the rapid fire of her thoughts. "Shall I return to the question after I sew up the Y incision?"

"I can sew it up," Haley said. "And yes, I'd be happy to go to dinner with you."

Dr. Palmer's face lit up. "Fabulous."

Before Haley's cheeks could flare with a red blush, they were interrupted by a knock on the door.

"Come in," Dr. Palmer bellowed. He moved to the sink to wash his hands as a police officer with thinning hair stepped inside, his helmet in one hand and a French Furet camera in the other.

"I'm Sergeant Scott," the officer announced. "I'm here to take photographs of the deceased, if that's all right with you."

"We're just finishing our initial examination," Dr. Palmer said. "A report will follow, but please take whatever photographs you need."

"Just of the face," Sergeant Scott clarified. "For identification purposes."

"Do you know who our unknown woman is?" Haley asked.

"Not so far, miss," the sergeant said. "We're going to show her face around. Hopefully, someone will recognise her."

Haley washed and took care of the paperwork associated with the post-mortem. After half a dozen shots of the body, Sergeant Scott excused himself. Haley covered the corpse's face with the sheet and then pushed it into the refrigerated cupboard. Turning back, she caught Dr. Palmer watching her, then quickly looking away.

Haley held back a smile as she pushed a curl behind her ear. She couldn't remember the last time she'd been on a date. She was looking forward to this one.

6

*B*asil studied the photographs spread out on the pockmarked surface of his wooden desk. Black-and-white images, more accurately shades of grey, with shadows that obscured the truth—at least, that was how Basil felt as frustration grew in his chest. Wouldn't it be wonderful if it were easier to photograph in colour? Would a vital clue jump out at him then?

The lifeless faces of the three street victims stared back at him, with only the two puncture wounds in youthful necks to offer a clue. Nothing in the surrounding area pointed to the identity of the would-be killer. No, assuming it was a man, this man hadn't left a trace of himself at the scenes. There were no dropped lighters, unfinished, snuffed-out cigarettes, or forgotten gloves or scarves. A meticulous killer. Which could be a clue in its own right. Perhaps the killer was used to working in a sterile environment or was simply a stickler for tidiness.

Nor were there any witnesses. At least any with the courage to come forward. These women had been found by bobbies who drew the short straw and patrolled the nastier parts of the city, where rats were more at home than humans and sinister, unlawful activities were performed under the cloak of darkness. Those areas had gas lamps that shed poor light when they worked at all.

Basil sighed. Sometimes he felt like he was fighting a losing battle. Crime was mightier than the law. Mightier than the weak and feeble, without protection or anyone to fight for their fundamental rights, like the right to live.

This was the reason Basil hadn't hung up his hat. He could live a life of leisure if he so chose. With plenty of money and no shortage of clubs on offer for gentlemen of his ilk, he could sit back and enjoy life with an endless supply of cigars and good whisky.

Another sigh followed as he picked up a photograph. This victim was only sixteen, still a child, and already shackled with a life of service to the whims of reprobate men. What would've happened to her had she escaped the clutches of this one? Would her life have been worth living? Or had providence done her a favour?

It wasn't for him to judge, not on how this girl had ended up a prostitute or on the quality of her life. It was hers to live, and this killer had stolen that from her.

And now there was another. Basil leaned back in his chair and rubbed the back of his neck. His mind was back at Madame Tussaud's wax museum, in the Dracula exhibit. Why this deviation from the pattern? The other three women were found outside —one in a ditch, one in a public house garden, and one under the overhang of a bridge.

The redness of the room was overpowering his recollection. Even the victim had been clothed in a turn-of-the-century gown of red velvet trimmed in black lace. Blond hair, a wig, he'd been told, in a Gibson girl style. This was a change in pattern, as the women in the photographs had been dumped as if they were rubbish. The only apparent effort on the killer's part had been to place the bodies on their backs so the neck wounds would not be missed.

Basil checked his wristwatch. He'd sent an officer to the mortuary to take a few more photographs of the corpse, but the ones taken that morning at the scene should be ready soon.

As if his thoughts conjured up reality, a tap on the door was followed by the entrance of an officer with an envelope in hand.

"The museum?" Basil asked as he stood to reach for it.

"Yes, sir. As you instructed, a team has already been dispatched to the streets with a facial shot."

Basil hoped for a quick identification. He nodded, excusing the officer, and settled back into his chair. He swooped the photographs on his desk into a neat pile and emptied the envelope contents.

A series of photographs produced the grey version of the crime scene and close-ups of the poor woman. Who was she? And how did she end up there?

After placing the photographs on the desk, Basil stretched out his long legs, then did the same with his arms, the crease of his white shirt wrinkling at the shoulders, his starched collar chafing his neck.

What he needed was a cuppa. Basil was on his feet as quickly as the thought came to him. Usually, he'd call for one of the constables, or desk clerks, to round up a pot of tea, but feeling restless, he headed to the staff area to set to the task himself. It sometimes helped, with a difficult case, to keep the hands busy with the mundane so the mind could work in the background. As Basil waited for the water to boil, he put tea leaves into a teapot, collected a teacup and saucer, and searched the new refrigerator the Met had recently acquired for some milk, only to find the bottle had been returned with barely a drop in it.

Blast the lazy sod who did that.

At least the gas ring worked splendidly, and the water soon boiled. Basil poured it into the pot and put his cup and saucer on a tray. He added a second cup and saucer and then returned with the tray to his office. Basil was dismayed that the domestic exercise hadn't worked a miracle on his subconscious and given him the key to this perplexing case.

Settling in at his desk, he poured his cup of tea and blew on it before taking a sip. He then took the pile of photographs he'd pushed to the side and selected close face and neck shots of each woman, putting them side by side next to the most recent one. They were silent now, but one of them had to speak somehow.

He heard Ginger's voice cheerily greeting the officers in reception as she passed them by. Basil felt a smile tug on his face. He hadn't expected his wife to show up, but he wasn't surprised. He was glad he'd obeyed the impulse to bring a second cup and saucer.

"Hello, darling," he said as she strolled in. He stepped towards her and kissed her on the cheek, feeling heady as his lips brushed her soft skin. The scent of flowers swirled from her perfume. His wife was a stylish, fashionable lady who took pride in her appearance, and her beauty and grace had first caught his attention nearly five years earlier on a journey across the Atlantic. He'd soon learned that a sharp and analytical mind lay beneath her glamorous exterior, which had only intensified his attraction to her.

"Hello, love." Ginger waved to the tea tray and the empty second cup. "Were you expecting someone?"

Basil poured as Ginger took the empty chair in front of his desk. "Would you believe me if I said 'you'?"

"I'd hate to think I've become that predictable." Ginger wrinkled her adorable nose. She accepted the cup when Basil held it out to her. "Thank you."

Sitting, Basil asked, "I think I know what brings you here. Unfortunately, I can't say I've learned anything new."

Ginger picked up the photograph of the latest victim, then nodded at the remaining three. "Do you know who they are?"

"We only know these three women by their street names. My men are working to find next of kin, but sadly—"

"—Many of these women are without family, or at least families willing to provide for them," Ginger said, finishing for him. "Which is why they're forced to do the only thing left to do to survive." She tutted. "Women should be given access to education as men are. I'm thankful my father saw that my sister and I had a thorough education."

"Your rather extensive inheritance is also a help," Basil said.

"Yes, I understand that I'm privileged as a woman in that regard as well, but I haven't squandered it. I work. I employ other women. I help those in need of help." Ginger set the photo down. "Which is why I'm here. I want to help these women and hopefully prevent others like them from suffering the same fate."

Basil had to admire his wife's tenacity. Even if her hopes and dreams for her sex were a little far-fetched. Then again, he'd never thought he'd see the day when women got the vote, and here they were. He, for one, was glad of it.

"What do we know for sure?" Ginger said. "You must have a list of suspects?"

"Our man has done us a favour with his latest antics. With these other women, the suspect list was every man who's ever walked through Villiers Street. But now ..."

"Now we can narrow it down to who had access to the museum before hours," Ginger said, "though that still allows for many options."

"Arthur Keene, the museum manager, is a place to start," Basil said. "And Horace Mathers, the wax figure artist who apparently worked on that exhibit."

"His figurine had been stuffed into the wardrobe," Ginger said. "I suppose the artist might do that if he thought it'd throw the scent off him."

Basil placed his empty teacup into its saucer with a clink. "Or it could've been the caretaker or any number of other folks. We need a definitive lead, or I fear we'll be chasing our proverbial tails."

"Perhaps Haley and her handsome doctor will discover something useful in the post-mortem."

Basil raised a brow as he grinned at his wife. Ginger loved to play cupid. "Palmer is Haley's handsome doctor now, is he?"

Ginger's slender shoulder lifted. "Why not? He seems to like her, and I can tell that Haley feels a certain attraction."

"Isn't she planning to return to America?" Basil asked.

"Nothing is set in stone, love."

There was a knock at the door, and Braxton stepped inside. "Good day, Mrs. Reed," he said before addressing Basil. "I'm sorry to interrupt, sir, but I thought you'd like to know the fellows have got a name for your unknown victim. Apparently, she's known in the area as Dinah Oakley."

"A street worker?" Basil asked.

Braxton nodded. "Worked at the Swan House, which is also a known opium den. An Annie Camden identified her. Annie was rather broken up by the news."

Basil reached for his suit jacket and shrugged it on. Ginger was already on her feet.

"I'm coming with you," she said.

Basil didn't even attempt to argue. "I know you are, love."

7

*G*inger regretted her clothing choice. The royal-blue wool coat with its light grey fur collar didn't allow her to blend in whilst she walked through Villiers Street with Basil by her side.

Villiers Street ran alongside Charing Cross Station from the Strand, close to the theatre district with its music halls and public houses. Men and women who found themselves destitute lived under the Adelphi Arches and Charing Cross Arches. Odd jobs and street begging were as common as prostitution was. Rooms were rented in the surrounding hotels and lodging houses by the hour.

Plain-clothed detectives and uniformed officers

patrolled the area. However, this didn't keep Basil from staying close to Ginger's side, as if he wanted to hold on to her but was resisting, knowing she'd have none of his misplaced gallantries. He tensed as the vagrants and scantily clad women subtly or sometimes blatantly hawked their wares. She gave her husband a knowing look of reassurance. She was more prepared than most ladies to defend herself, though he didn't know exactly why.

Although perhaps he did. Ginger had been sworn to secrecy, but Basil was astute and had likely concluded that she'd served their country during the war in a clandestine way she wasn't free to discuss. He would press her for answers if he hadn't, but lately, he had let the topic lie, fat like a roast pig never to be carved and eaten.

Basil had a photograph of Dinah Oakley in his hands, presenting her in the best light as if she were sleeping and not dead. He and Ginger approached individuals who loitered about, Basil with his arm reaching out, presenting the face of Miss Oakley.

"Do you know this woman?" he asked, not because he needed further identification but because he wanted to discover more information about her. The man in question looked respectable enough in a well-worn suit and trilby hat. He wrinkled his nose. "The tarts all look alike to me. Why? She in trouble?"

"You could say that," Basil said. "Do you know a gal called Annie Camden?"

The man lifted his bristled chin. "That's 'er over there, poor thing. I'm told she's grievin' after losin' a dear one."

Ginger's gaze shot to the woman sitting on the house steps. Young, barely in her twenties, she wore an outdated frock with a floral shawl thrown over thin shoulders. She held a handkerchief to her face. A man, strolling by with hands in his trouser pockets, whistled at her, hoping to get her attention.

Ginger's heart jumped with recognition. She grabbed Basil's arm. "Isn't that Alfred Schofield?"

Alfred Schofield was the grandson of Ginger's neighbour Mrs. Schofield. They'd been introduced after Ginger had moved back to Hartigan House. He'd promised to call in often to check on his grandmother, but from what Ginger had seen over the previous four years, it was a promise he'd broken. Alfred had been a lieutenant in the Royal Flying Corps during the Great War.

Basil squinted, lines deepening further around his hazel eyes as his jaw tensed. "Is he soliciting?"

"Oh mercy," Ginger said. "I hope not. I wonder how long he's been back in London?"

Basil cast her a look. "Where has he been?"

"I really don't know. I haven't seen him for donkey's years, and Mrs. Schofield hasn't spoken about him. In fact, I just saw Mrs. Schofield today, and she didn't mention him."

"Perhaps she doesn't know he's back."

"Or perhaps it briefly slipped her mind. She and Ambrosia were in a rather serious discussion."

"Oh? Tea and scone preferences?" Basil asked lightly as they started walking towards Alfred and Annie.

"If only the topic were so benign. They were engaged in a political conversation about the Macmillan Report, and both are eagerly canvassing for Gerald Hall."

This news elicited a whistle from Basil just as Alfred Schofield caught sight of them. Instead of acknowledging their presence, Alfred pulled down on the brim of his hat and hotfooted it in the opposite direction.

"I suppose he has a right to embarrassment," Ginger said.

"I'm more inclined to see it as a response to guilt."

At least Annie Camden didn't dart away when she saw them. Her shoulders drooped, and she sighed as if she felt defeated. The pale skin of her face looked nearly translucent, despite her having added two striking red circles of rouge on her cheeks. Her hair, short like nearly every other woman in London, perhaps the developed world, hung limp and unwashed. Her bloodshot eyes landed on Basil. "Yer a copper?"

With a quick nod, Basil said, "You were friends with Dinah Oakley?"

Annie sniffed. "Cor blimey. Dinah was one of the bleedin' good'uns. She didn't deserve to snuff it."

"I'm very sorry for your loss," Ginger said.

Annie looked Ginger up and down. Her eyes settled on Ginger's coat's fur trim as she tightened her own arms around her chest against the cold.

"This is Lady Gold," Basil said. "She's a private investigator and occasionally consults with the Met."

"A lady sleuth-hound, eh?" Annie snorted. "Don't spect to see the loikes of yer int'rested in my sort."

"I only see a woman in distress," Ginger said kindly, "over a female friend who's been unjustly murdered." She sat on the bench beside Annie, continuing, "In this regard, we are the same *sort*."

Annie's expression softened. "Oi do apologise,

me dear. It's just so frightenin'. If someone would do that to Dinah, well then, none of us is safe, is we?"

"Who was that man you were talking to?" Basil asked.

Miss Camden's gaze darted in the direction Alfred Schofield had fled. "'E's one of Dinah's, ain't he."

"Was he asking for her?" Ginger asked gently. She disliked Alfred Schofield, but she did hold a fondness for his grandmother. If Alfred had been asking for Dinah, that could imply he wasn't the killer.

"Nah. 'E wanted me to come wiv 'im, but I ain't gonna step on Dinah's turf before she's even cold in 'er bleedin' grave."

"Did Miss Oakley ever mention feeling afraid for her life?" Ginger asked. "Was there a client she disliked? Someone unkind to her?"

Annie scoffed. "Cor blimey, we's all scared, luv. Who fancies us anyway? Yer gotta know someone to like 'em, and well, the sorta folks we's entertainin' ain't really lookin' to know us like that." She glanced at Basil, and her eyes widened in horror. "Yer ain't gonna nick me, are yer? I'm bleedin' confused. I dunno what's comin' outta me gob."

"No," Basil said. "I'm not interested in arresting

you or any of your friends. I'm a homicide detective. I'm only concerned with finding Dinah Oakley's killer."

Fear flashed behind Miss Camden's eyes. "And the other girls."

Basil nodded. "Where can we find you should we have any more questions regarding this matter?"

"I'm stayin' at the Swan 'Ouse, as yer probably know." Miss Camden shivered as she got to her feet. "I really should be goin'. A workin' bird's gotta stuff 'er face, yer know."

Ginger stood as well and placed a hand on Annie's arm. "Miss Camden, I'm wondering if you know anyone who'd be interested in this coat? I was thinking this morning that I might get another one. I could throw it away, but . . ."

Annie eyed Ginger's royal-blue coat greedily. "I could find someone who'd wear it for yer if it's going in the rubbish bin anyway."

Ginger slipped the coat off and handed it to Annie. "Thank you, Miss Camden. I do hate things going to waste before their time."

Annie hurried down the footpath, only getting a few feet away before thrusting her skinny arms into the sleeves and snuggling into the warmth of the fur collar.

When Ginger turned back to Basil, she found him staring at her with adoration. He removed his overcoat and placed it over her shoulders. "Shall we head home, love?"

8

*G*inger was pleased when she found Haley in the morning room, just sitting down for breakfast.

"Good morning," Ginger said as she picked up a plate from the stack on the sideboard. Mrs. Beasley always dished up a delightful breakfast of grilled kippers, bacon, and scrambled eggs, kept warm in the chafing dish.

"The fish is delicious," Haley said. "I think I'm adapting to the English breakfast palate."

Ginger took a seat across the table. The morning room was bright, with sunlight coming through long French windows. Outside, colourful spring flowers trimmed the back garden.

"Any news from the mortuary about our latest victim—"

"Dinah Oakley," Haley said. "We got word at the mortuary last night. She suffered bruising along her arms and thighs—"

"—A sign of a struggle?" Ginger interjected.

"Possibly, though, women in her line of work often suffer bruising due to rough-playing clientele. Dr. Palmer believes she was poisoned, as do I. We're waiting on blood-testing results."

Ginger's face softened to a playful grin at the mention of the doctor. "How's it going with Dr. Palmer?"

"I'm sure I don't know what you mean," Haley returned stiffly.

Ginger laughed. "Your answer proves you do know what I mean."

"Fine. He asked me out. I said yes, but now I'm conflicted."

"Why are you conflicted?"

"Because, as much as I love London, I plan to return to Boston. My brother's murder case is cold, and I can't leave it as such."

Sadly, Haley's brother Joseph Higgins had been a victim of a violent crime, and the guilty party remained at large. Haley had left suddenly after his death while still a student at the London Medical School for Women.

"You can still go for dinner," Ginger said lightly. "It's not a marriage proposal. One can never have too many friends at one's side."

"I suppose." Haley exhaled exaggeratedly. Changing the subject, she asked, "Has Basil left already?"

"Yes," Ginger said. "The poor man tossed and turned all night. This case is getting the better of him. Four women murdered, and no prime suspect. Though . . ."

Haley stopped mid-chew, raised a brow, and mouthed, "Though?"

"Basil and I visited Villiers Street yesterday in the late afternoon, hoping to find someone who knew Miss Oakley. We learned she'd had a good friend named Annie Camden, but when we spotted Miss Camden, she was being solicited by Alfred Schofield."

Haley lowered her coffee cup to the table. "Mrs. Schofield's grandson?"

"The same."

Haley snorted. "I haven't thought of the man since that fiasco with the skeleton in your attic."

"Me neither."

"I do recall he had eyes for you."

"And for Felicia," Ginger said with a scowl.

Haley snorted again. "A womaniser."

"And a two-timer," Ginger said. "You'll remember he was having a clandestine affair the whole time."

"With such a ferocious appetite, I suppose we shouldn't be surprised that he frequents brothels and the like."

"Who has a ferocious appetite?" Ambrosia's gravelly voice interrupted. "Or shall I say, who doesn't when it comes to the morning meal?"

Ginger got to her feet. "Allow me to serve you." Ginger was well versed in Ambrosia's breakfast preference. The dowager nodded as if the statement was unnecessary.

"Would you like me to pour you some tea?" Haley asked.

"That would be good, thank you," Ambrosia returned as she would to a servant. She wasn't a fan of Americans and distrusted any female who preferred trousers to a day frock.

After a sip of tea, Ambrosia said, "I hope Felicia and Charles return soon. It feels like they've been away for a long while."

"Didn't they go to Scotland?" Haley asked.

"Yes," Ginger answered. "I received a letter from

Felicia yesterday. She was quite thrilled to visit Slains Castle."

Ambrosia harrumphed. "One castle is the same as the next."

Ginger set a plate of breakfast in front of Ambrosia. "But this one apparently inspired Bram Stoker when he wrote *Dracula*. Felicia says it is set on the cliff overlooking the sea and has the most romantic turrets and weather-worn ruins." Ginger quite enjoyed Felicia's letters. Her skills as a mystery writer were evident. The way she described it all brought it to life in Ginger's imagination.

"If I remember correctly," Haley started, "Felicia had a fascination for Mr. Stoker. She was more than a little thrilled when you purchased a copy of *Dracula* for your library."

"I have little regard for such dark works," Ambrosia said, "and I hope Felicia will find a raison d'être immersing herself in charity work and other duties appropriate for a lady of her standing. She represents her husband now."

Ginger shared a look with Haley as she sipped her coffee. Ambrosia clung to old sentiments of what a woman's place was in the world.

"Did Felicia say when they're returning?"

Ambrosia asked. "It's so quiet around here without her."

"Perhaps next month," Ginger answered, "but I must agree that life is much duller without Felicia around. At least you have Mrs. Schofield to keep you company."

"She cheats at cards," Ambrosia said after she'd swallowed a fork full of eggs. "But she is enthusiastic about Mr. Hall. We're going to a rally at Trafalgar Square in a couple of weeks. You should come."

Ginger stared evenly at her grandmother-in-law, wondering if it would be worth stirring the pot by mentioning that she and Haley would likely be on the other side of the protest. She exhaled, keeping the contentious comment to herself. "Perhaps we will," she said instead. "That would be interesting, wouldn't it, Haley?"

Haley blinked. "It would?"

"Yes. Mr. Hall has taken a stand against the evils of prostitution. He might shed some light on our case."

Ambrosia huffed. "Must all table conversations revert to your work, Ginger? Surely, some topics must be considered unsuitable for discussion over a meal, even for you."

"I apologise, Grandmother." Ginger smiled,

hoping it came across as endearing. "Oh, guess who I saw in town yesterday. Alfred Schofield. Did you know he was back in London?"

Ambrosia harrumphed. "I get the impression her opinion of her grandson has diminished."

"Is that so?" Haley's eyes widened with interest. "She seemed overcome with pride for him when I met them in twenty-three."

"Yes, well, time changes things," Ambrosia said, "including our opinions. Young Alfred had served valiantly in the Great War, which is to be admired. However, how he's choosing to live now isn't something Mrs. Schofield wants to shed light on."

"How is he living his life now?" Ginger asked.

"It's only gossip, Ginger," Ambrosia said, "and you know I'm not one for gossip, but Mrs. Schofield has made a career out of it, so I'm unfortunately burdened with more information than I'd like. I'll pass the burden on to you."

Ginger nodded. Burden sharing, in Ambrosia's mind, did not equate to gossip.

"Alfred has a drug problem," Ambrosia continued. "Cocaine and the like."

"Unfortunately, that's not uncommon for many soldiers who've returned from France," Haley said.

"It was widely available there, and soldiers were encouraged to use it to buoy their courage."

"Where has he been all this time?" Ginger asked. "To my knowledge, he hasn't been to visit his grandmother, so I'm assuming he wasn't in London."

"Mrs. Schofield doesn't know. The Continent or America. However, it seems he's run out of money, so his interest in his grandmother has been renewed. He came back begging for a place to stay. Now, if you don't mind, I'd like to finish breakfast before it cools."

Haley excused herself. "I'm scheduled at the hospital today."

"Ring me when you hear from the laboratory," Ginger said.

"I will," Haley replied. To Ambrosia, she said, "Have a good day, Lady Gold."

"Thank you," Ambrosia returned politely.

Ginger finished her breakfast and enjoyed a second cup of coffee whilst Ambrosia ate. Conversation was kept to the weather and how it was almost time to wake up the garden, but Ginger's mind was on poor Dinah Oakley and her connection with Alfred Schofield.

"What are your plans for the day?" Ambrosia asked.

Usually, Ginger would check in at her shop, Feathers & Flair, or with Magna Jones, her assistant at her investigation office, but she heard herself saying something entirely different.

"I'm going back to Madame Tussaud's wax museum."

9

*G*inger had complete confidence in Madame Roux, her shop manager, to run the Regent Street store proficiently. Magna was kept busy with the growing number of people looking to prove their spouses were unfaithful so they might obtain a divorce. Indeed, the Autographic Kodak camera was getting good use.

Knowing this, Ginger diverted her plans without concern and returned to Madame Tussaud's wax museum. She parked her motorcar nearby, one front tyre resting on the edge of the pedestrian pavement. She wasn't sure what she hoped to accomplish by coming back, but another conversation with the manager, Mr. Keene, couldn't hurt.

The museum was eye-catching with its Gothic arches and intricate stone detailing. Tall turrets flanked the grand entrance archway which was topped with a spiky pinnacle. Pedestrians filling pavements on either side of Marylebone Road slowed their steps to admire the structure.

Unfortunately, Ginger didn't have the credentials to waltz inside without buying another ticket.

"Is Mr. Keene on the premises?" she asked before handing money to the ticket attendant.

"He is, indeed, and popular today."

"Oh?" Ginger said, taking her ticket from the man. "Others are enquiring after him?"

The man took a quick look over his shoulder, then lowered his voice. "It's not for me to say, but just as a warning to a fine lady like yourself, they were coppers."

Ginger nibbled her lip. Quite likely, it was Basil inside. He hadn't asked her officially to consult on this case, and she hoped he'd be all right with her poking her nose in.

"How long ago did the police come?" she asked.

"Only a few minutes before yourself, madam."

Ginger waved her ticket. "Since I've already bought a ticket, I'll take a tour through the exhibits until Mr. Keene is free. Where would one find his office?"

"It's upstairs, madam." Other patrons had lined up behind Ginger, and the ticket clerk's gaze moved past her. Ginger took the stairs to the upper level, where she found the manager's office, the door marked.

Ginger slowly pressed down on the door handle, which was conveniently unlocked. The latch quietly clicked, and the door opened a crack. Through it, Ginger could see Basil's back as he stared at a nervous-looking manager. Another man at a desk perpendicular to Mr. Keene's, presumably Mr. Keene's secretary, looked equally anxious. At Basil's side, Constable Braxton was scribbling on a small notepad with a stubby pencil.

"I honestly don't know how this could've happened, Chief Inspector. We've been working on the exhibits for months. Do you know how long it takes to make one, especially if it replicates a living, breathing person? For example, the work involved in producing a life-size, lifelike figure takes many hours of painstaking precision by masters in the field. Work is done in studios around the city; some are even imported from Paris."

"I can appreciate the artistry involved," Basil

said. "What about the figures based on fictional characters like Dracula and his nameless victim?"

"Those don't take as long," Mr. Keene said. "The artists involved with those are not masters, but proficient."

Basil lifted his chin. "Where do those artists create their work?"

"There is a studio in the basement." Mr. Keene motioned downward with his arm. "Along with costume storage and the like not currently being used."

"Do you know a Dinah Oakley, Mr. Keene?" Basil asked.

Mr. Keene sniffed. "Just in passing."

"Passing where?" Ginger asked.

The manager's eyes twitched. Instead of answering her, he turned back to Basil. "You know, where a *certain type* of woman loiters about." He nodded at Basil as if he would understand the emphasis. "On Villiers Street."

Mr. Keene's secretary's forehead buckled as he gave his boss a slight shake of the head. "Mr. Keene."

Mr. Keene looked back at the man deeply as if in silent communication. Turning back to Basil, he said, "Not that I have personal experience as to what goes on there, but it's hardly a secret."

Basil faced the secretary. "What about you, Mr. Lockhart? Were you acquainted with Dinah Oakley?"

Mr. Lockhart sniffed more indignantly than his boss had before him. "I most certainly did not. I'm too busy with work and taking care of Mr. Keene's needs to have time for that sort of thing."

Ginger raised a brow at the slight emphasis Mr. Lockhart had placed on the words "Mr. Keene's needs."

Basil thanked the men, looking to Ginger as if he'd given up on getting more clarifying information from either of them. He entered the corridor and stopped short in front of her. "Ginger?" His eyes narrowed as he stared at her knowingly. "I was going to ask what you're doing here, but I think I know."

"The door was already unlocked," she returned defensively. She patted her handbag where her set of lock picks remained safely stored. "I can't help it if I happened to witness your interrogation."

Basil stepped beside her as she headed back down the stairs, Constable Braxton staying a few steps behind them. "It wasn't an interrogation," Basil returned. "I was simply asking a few questions."

"What did you learn?" Ginger asked.

Basil let out a short breath. "Nothing new.

Neither Keene nor his secretary, Lockhart, admits to knowing Dinah Oakley, but I hardly expect any man to do so willingly, not to the police."

"Did they seem rather . . . close?" Ginger asked.

"The way their desks were situated is the usual formation for a man in authority and his secretary. It makes it easy for one to communicate with the other."

"I'm quite aware of that, love. Magna and I have the same set-up in my office."

"Yes, of course," Basil returned. "Then what do you mean?"

"I mean, it seemed they were rather emotionally connected."

Basil stopped, and Ginger paused with him. "Do you mean romantically?"

"It wouldn't be the first time such a thing has happened." Ginger started walking again, and Basil followed, Constable Braxton still keeping a couple of steps behind them. When they got to the bottom of the stairs, Ginger didn't slow, and Basil added, "Wait, where are you going?"

"To the basement." Ginger glanced over her shoulder, nodding for Basil to follow. "We need to talk to the artist who made the figurine we found stuffed in the wardrobe."

. . .

"Horace Mathers, at your service," the man returned after Basil had introduced himself and Ginger, ignoring Constable Braxton, who stood off to the side. The museum's basement was frightening in its own way, with shelves of porcelain body parts, wigs, and costumes. The dim lighting made it look like a dreadful crime scene or the fictional imagination of a dangerous mind.

"How did you find yourself in such an interesting line of work, Mr. Mathers?" Ginger asked. "A fine artist must've had plenty of options."

The man's face rounded as he smiled, his eyes nearly disappearing. "I'm a student of many masters. But honestly, there weren't many paying jobs for artists after the war. I was repairing statues and monuments when Mr. Keene found me. Like most citizens of London, I was devastated when the museum burned and delighted when I heard it would be rebuilt. It's an honour to be part of history."

Mr. Mathers obviously spent much time alone with his work, and Ginger felt he enjoyed a chance for a chinwag.

"It's my understanding that you worked on the Dracula exhibit," Basil said.

After an enthusiastic nod, Mr. Mathers said,

"Though many works involve producing lifelike replicas of real persons, I prefer being guided by my imagination."

"You must've been shocked to hear that one of your pieces had been unceremoniously shoved into a wardrobe," Ginger said.

"Indeed, I was, madam. But I can salvage the piece." Mr. Mathers shrugged like a man used to bearing the weight of a demanding job. "Once the police release it back to the museum."

"I'm afraid it might be tied up in evidence for some time," Basil said.

"That doesn't matter," Mr. Mathers said lightly. "I can create another one."

"Did you know the victim?" Basil asked.

Mr. Mathers shook his head dramatically. "I certainly did not."

Ginger shot Basil a glance at the artist's overly exertive denial. "A Miss Dinah Oakley?"

"No, madam," Mr. Mathers insisted. A red blush crept up his neck, and he pulled at his collar. He either found the room warm or wasn't very good at lying.

"She resided at the Swan House," Basil said. "We understand if you wished to keep your visits there quiet and any association discreet. However, this is a murder investigation, and if I discover you're with-holding information, you could be charged with obstruction of justice."

Mr. Mathers dug his heels in. "As I said, I didn't know the woman. I'm very sorry for her demise, but the rest of us still have work to do."

Ginger spotted Basil's jaw tightening at the man's barely veiled dismissal.

"We'll let you get back to it, then," Basil said, "but we might be around to ask questions again in the future."

Mr. Mathers blew heavily through his nose in relief. Before climbing the steps, Ginger asked the man a final question. "Are you married, Mr. Mathers?"

"Indeed, madam. And happily!"

Once they had left the museum, Basil turned to Ginger. "What did you think of that?"

"I think many men visit Villiers Street and don't wish anyone to know about it, especially their wives. I believe Mr. Mathers is lying about that, but just because he visits the Swan House doesn't mean he was personally acquainted with Miss Oakley."

"It doesn't mean he wasn't either," Basil said with a note of frustration. "Every man who crossed the threshold could be a suspect."

"Well, not every man," Ginger countered. "He would need to access the museum."

"There's a back door used by plenty of tradesmen. One would only need to disguise oneself and carry the body like a prop."

Ginger had to concede Basil had a point. "Speaking of any man, it appears that Alfred Schofield is again our neighbour. Ambrosia said that he's recently moved in with his grandmother. Apparently, Mrs. Schofield isn't thrilled."

Basil checked his wristwatch. "Perhaps lunch at Hartigan House is in order. Then we could call in next door."

Ginger took Basil's arm. "That's a frightfully good idea, love."

*a*s serendipity would have it, Mrs. Schofield was at Hartigan House for another visit with Ambrosia. With Alfred residing again with his grandmother, Ginger understood why Ambrosia was hosting their tête-à-têtes.

"Mr. Hall is the man we need." Ambrosia tightened her lips with a settled look as Ginger and Basil walked in. Her bulbous eyes grew even rounder when she spotted them. "Isn't that so, Basil? I would think the Metropolitan Police would favour a man on the council willing to go the extra mile to clean up the streets."

Mrs. Schofield blew a soft raspberry through her lips as she nodded in agreement. "Prostitution is a blight on modern society." Her small eyes seemed to disappear around folds of skin. "Don't you agree?"

"There are many injustices in the world," Ginger said to placate the ladies. She smiled at her neighbour. "Is it true that your grandson is back in the city?"

The light of zeal in Mrs. Schofield's eyes dimmed. "It is, Mrs. Reed. He's opted to stay with me for a while."

"It must be nice to have a young man around the house again."

Mrs. Schofield offered a hum of noncommitment. "A wife and children would do him good. He favours lounging around in bed for a long time most mornings."

"Surely he must be awake by now," Ginger said. "Basil and I would love to drop in to say 'hello'."

"I served with his brother," Basil said gently, "if you recall."

"Oh, poor Angus," Mrs. Schofield said. "The war took all the good ones. I'll never get over his death."

"Will you come to the rally, Ginger?" Ambrosia asked. She was like a dog with a bone these days when it came to her latest cause.

Ginger hedged. "I'm not very political."

"Oh, poppycock!" Ambrosia blustered. "The Great War has made politicians out of us all."

"I'll give it some thought," Ginger offered. "It's nice to see you again, Mrs. Schofield."

After a lovely but brisk lunch of chicken soup and thick slices of buttered bread, Ginger told Digby they would be stepping out again, and he returned with their hats and coats.

Digby was a sturdy sort who was just old enough to have missed war action. Though shorter than Pippins, he stood upright and at attention and was every bit as efficient and conscientious. After a slight bow, he asked, "Do you need anything else, madam? Sir?"

Ginger smiled graciously and said, "That's all for now, thank you."

Ginger and Basil stepped out the front entrance and down the stone path to the wrought-iron fence that divided the front garden from the street. There were only a handful of houses in the cul-de-sac, all rather grand limestone structures with two or more storeys and larger-than-normal grounds for properties found in the city. Felicia and Charles had acquired the one across from Hartigan House, and Mrs. Schofield occupied the one next door.

Basil used the door knocker and the Schofield

maid opened the front door. Her eyes brightened with recognition. With a curtsy, she said, "Good afternoon, madam, sir."

"Good afternoon," Ginger said. "We're here to call on Mr. Schofield."

"He's having tea in the morning room," the maid said. "If you'll follow me to the sitting room, I'll fetch him for you."

The sitting room looked the same as the previous time Ginger had visited. An abundance of mid-Victorian furniture, which looked as old as its owner, filled the area, and plenty of garish paintings hung on darkly papered walls.

Alfred arrived looking a little worse for wear. His former boyish good looks were quickly disappearing, with new wrinkles on his forehead and circles around his eyes.

"Please forgive my appearance," he said sheepishly, dropping into the armchair and crossing his legs. "I had a rather late night." A length of his hair had fallen over his forehead, and he pushed it back with a smooth swipe of his hand. Ginger noted the slight tremor. He grinned crookedly at her. "Good to see you again, Lady Gold. It's been some time, hasn't it?"

"Indeed. I'm Mrs. Reed now. The Chief Inspector and I have married in the meantime."

"I see." Alfred's bloodshot eyes narrowed in Basil's direction. "I'd heard something about that. Swooped in for the 'gold', didn't you, old chap?"

Though Ginger had taken a seat, Basil remained standing. Ignoring the jibe, he said, "Villiers Street. Was that where you were late last night?"

Alfred snorted as he hauled himself upright. Placing his elbows on his knees, he stared up. "I suspected this wasn't a good-hearted social call, but I don't know what you're on about. I was at Merriweather's Club. Despite nasty rumours that might be circulated about me, I don't frequent Villiers Street."

"But Mr. Schofield," Ginger started, "we saw you there. With our own eyes."

"That wasn't me."

Basil shot Alfred a sideways glance. "You weren't conversing with a woman known as Annie Camden?"

Alfred sniffed and tucked his shaky hands under his armpits. "No, sir."

"If I were to call on the gentlemen's club, would I find someone to verify your story?"

"What story?" Alfred's eyes darted quickly

between Ginger and Basil. "What's this about? Why am I being so rudely questioned?"

"Alfred," Ginger said gently. "A woman's been murdered, and we've been told you are a, uh, an occasional companion. We're looking for people who last saw her alive."

Alfred huffed as he relaxed back into his chair. "Sorry to hear about the poor gal, but I'm afraid you're barking up the wrong tree."

"The name Dinah Oakley doesn't ring a bell?" Basil asked.

Alfred blinked. "Dinah?"

"Miss Oakley," Ginger said. "Did you know her?"

"Oh, no," Alfred said. "I don't know a Dinah." He pushed himself out of his chair. "Now, if you'll excuse me, my stomach's not quite right. I'd offer tea, but it would be better for us all if I returned to bed."

"Thank you so much for your time," Ginger said, standing. "We can show ourselves out."

Outside, Ginger took Basil's arm as they headed to their house next door. "I don't think he knew her last name," Ginger said. "But he definitely knows someone by the name of Dinah."

11

Basil left Ginger at Hartigan House. Rosa had awakened from her nap, and Ginger was keen to spend time with her. Basil would've liked to stay longer, too, but his case had become an incessant itch that demanded scratching. Four dead women. Basil desperately hoped there wouldn't be a fifth yet felt helpless to stop the monster. Basil huffed as he slapped the steering wheel of his Austin. With no proof and little in the way of suspects, he felt like a pawn in the killer's deadly game.

And as always, Ginger insisted on inserting herself in the case. If there was one thing he knew about his wife, she would not be dictated to. She had a bloated sense of her ability to protect herself—at least in his opinion—and not nearly enough natural fear. If he'd warned her against this lunatic and shown her the letter implying potential danger, Ginger wouldn't have cowered. She would've got her hackles up and risen to the challenge. If he'd mentioned the personal attack, Ginger would have been sitting next to him in his Austin, with that look of determination Basil knew so well, instead of playing with their daughter in the safety of their own house.

He had jolly well done the right thing by not telling her.

Though he'd be naive to think Ginger would lounge about the house all day. There was always something that brought her into the dangerous streets of London. It would be best if he could just wrap up this case, find the killer, and throw away the key.

The traffic slowed as Basil reached Trafalgar Square. Drivers of the motorcars and double-decker motor buses squeezed their horns and pumped puffs of smoke as they idled along. Horses whinnied, displeased at being crowded out by the noisy machines, irritating their cart drivers by tossing up their heads, or worse, releasing a dung pile.

Blast it.

Craning his neck, he discovered the problem's source: that radical politician Gerald Hall. Rallies with more than a dozen people were illegal, but the man believed any publicity was good publicity. However, until the police arrived to disband the crowd, Basil couldn't just stand by. He found a place to park his Austin and then ran towards the disturbance.

Mr. Hall's voice carried from his position in front of the base of Nelson's column. "Vote for me, and I promise to do everything in my power to clean up the streets of London, once and for all. No more prostitution. No more crime! Vote for a strong council!"

Another crowd had formed across the square. This group—all women—held placards and shouted. One taller woman stood at the front, the apparent leader.

"Women are not dogs to be penned and managed! We want equality! Full voting rights for women!"

Basil knew who she was since she'd been arrested for public disturbance on multiple occasions. She kept being released only because she came from a respectable family of means and had proficient knowledge of the law.

"Miss Forbes," Basil shouted. "You know the law. You mustn't disturb the public."

Helen Forbes pointed at Gerald Hall. "And what about him? Is he not doing the same? Why come to me first?"

"I'm coming from the direction of my vehicle, and it's only by chance that I've reached you first. The police have been notified and will arrive shortly." Basil could only assume this as he hadn't rung the police himself, but the clanging sounds of police bells approaching supported his words. "Do yourself and these ladies a favour by dispersing before you all find yourself in cuffs again."

Miss Forbes lifted her chin. "How's Mrs. Reed?"

Basil, caught out by the sudden change in topic, particularly the reference to his wife, paused before saying, "She's fine. Now . . ."

"She sides with us, you know," Miss Forbes continued. "She'd have been here if she'd known."

Basil held in a sigh. He didn't doubt Miss Forbes' words. "It's a good thing she didn't know. Now I insist, in the name of the law, take your placards and go home."

Miss Forbes snorted defiantly. "I'll go when he goes."

Thankfully, the police arrived. Mr. Hall wasn't as

willing to go to jail for his cause and lifted his hands in faux surrender. "We'll leave peacefully, officers," he said with a loud chuckle. "You can put those batons away."

Once Mr. Hall and his supporters moved out of the square, Miss Forbes rallied her troop of women and marched in the opposite direction. Basil hoofed it back to his Austin, relieved to find the traffic was jostling ahead. He motored to the Yard quickly, hoping that Braxton or one of the other officers would have some news for him that would help break this case. He'd like nothing more than to catch a killer before the day was over.

Basil, removing his hat as politeness dictated, entered the Scotland Yard building. He was part way through the reception area when he spotted Lockhart sitting on the wooden bench. The secretary wore a neatly pressed suit with a colourful tie, and his hair was trimmed and tamed. His legs were crossed at the knee, and he cupped his hands on his lap. At this short distance, Basil noticed the man's long, slender fingers with well-manicured nails.

"Mr. Lockhart?"

He glanced up at Basil with a flash of misery in his eyes, then stood. "Chief Inspector. I wasn't sure if I should come."

"Well, now you're here," Basil said. "Would you like to speak to me in my office?"

The man nodded, and Basil led the way. Basil motioned to the empty chair in front of his desk, then took his own seat. Once they were both seated, Basil asked, "Do you have some news for me?"

"Nothing extraordinary, I'm afraid." Lockhart played nervously with his hat. "I probably shouldn't be here, but . . ." He defiantly lifted his chin. "Mr. Keene wasn't being truthful. He most certainly visited the Swan House."

"I see." Basil leaned back in his chair. "I suppose the question remains, was Mr. Keene involved with Miss Oakley?"

Lockhart's expression flattened. "That I wouldn't know."

"Why are you telling me this, Mr. Lockhart? Wouldn't Mr. Keene's arrest interrupt your career? Or are you in line to become the next manager?"

Lockhart huffed. "I should've known better than to come. Here I thought that I was helping the police, and the first thing you do is turn it around on me. Very typical."

"I appreciate you taking the time to come and see me, Mr. Lockhart," Basil said. "I most certainly do. But you must understand the difficulty of my job.

For instance, how do I know that you're not the one who visited the Swan House to be entertained by Dinah Oakley?" The question was a test. Basil didn't have to wait long for the results.

Lockhart dropped his chin. "I can assure you I'm not the type to visit such establishments." He looked up at Basil and held his eye. "I'm simply not interested in that sort of thing."

Basil nodded as he broke their gaze. Ginger's instincts had been spot-on. Basil couldn't expect Lockhart to come right out and admit something illegal in the eyes of British law, but if true, it would erase motive, at least one of passionate intimacy with women who lived at the Swan House.

"Is there anything else you'd like to report, Mr. Lockhart?"

Lockhart jumped to his feet. "No, sir. And if I might make a request, please don't inform my employer of my visit here."

"I can promise you that, as long as it's not needed to settle this case."

Lockhart dipped his chin, his shoulders slumping as if weighted with what he'd done. Whatever had spurred him to betray his boss was unknown to Basil, and nothing could change the fact now.

12

*H*artigan House was one of the first private residences in London to have a telephone. Ginger had since replaced the older-style candlestick version with a wall-mounted one in the corridor and had added a black rotary model, which sat conveniently on her desk in the study. Most government institutions, like police stations and hospitals, now had telephones, and many businesses were also modernising their communication abilities this way. Ginger had had one installed at both her dress shop and her investigative office.

With Basil gone and Rosa in Nanny Green's care, Ginger took a cup of tea into her study—once her father's study—to attend to some business matters from home. As in all rooms with fireplaces, a dog bed sat on the floor near to the hearth. After following Ginger into the room, Boss, her black and white Boston Terrier, curled up on it, then immediately fell asleep.

Her desk had stacks of fashion magazines and the latest catalogues selling fabric and accessories. Ginger made it her mission to be on top of the latest popular fabrics and designs and always had them on offer to her customers.

She paid bills by stuffing cheques into envelopes and produced invoices using her Underwood typewriter, later handing them to Digby to put in the post.

Picking up her telephone receiver, Ginger dialled the operator and gave the number for her investigations office. She was pleased when she heard Magna's voice on the line.

"Lady Gold Investigations," Magna said dryly. "Miss Jones here. How may I help you?"

Ginger could picture her stiff-necked assistant: chin up, lips pursed, and dark, glossy hair cut severely short along the back of her neck. Magna was as no-nonsense as they came, and her work ethic and machine-like efficiency made up for her lack of congeniality.

"Magna, it's Ginger."

"Ringing? I expected you to call in at the office in person today. Is everything all right?"

"Yes, everything is hunky-dory. I'm working from home this afternoon. I was just wondering, did you succeed with your assignment?"

"I did," Magna said.

"Did he see you?" Ginger asked, regretting it the moment the words left her mouth. She prepared herself for the reprimand that would most surely follow.

"Of course not! I'm not a novice."

"My apologies, I—"

"I've got photographs. The target not only engaged a woman but also entered the establishment."

"I see."

Ginger was both pleased and dismayed at the news. She'd have to tell Basil what she'd done— Magna had followed Alfred Schofield. She and Basil shared a similar vocation, and her husband sometimes asked for her assistance in the official capacity as a police consultant. It was a privileged position based on her past work, thankfully, and not her relationship with Basil, though he was her firm advocate when others took a dim view of her presence. Superintendent Morris had reluctantly agreed to allow

Ginger to contribute, since he'd been the personal recipient of Ginger's investigative prowess on more than one occasion.

Except with this case, Basil hadn't asked for her help. In fact, he'd asked for the opposite and implied that he wished for her to stay indoors.

Asking Magna to follow a suspect would be frowned upon, but now that Ginger had information, it was imperative that she share it.

"Is there anything else you'd like me to do?" Magna asked.

"How deep is the proof of infidelity file?" Divorce in Britain was only allowed when infidelity could be proved. Ginger and Magna were often employed by spouses, primarily wives, looking for a way out of an unhappy marriage.

"About six deep," Magna said. "A new one came in today. A woman by the name of Bernice Mathers."

"Mathers?" Ginger straightened in her chair. "Married to Horace Mathers, who works at the wax museum?"

"The one and the same. The timing is a strange coincidence, isn't it?"

"Indeed. And he made a point of claiming to be happily married."

Magna snorted. "Happily unfaithful. Mrs.

Mathers suspects he's a regular visitor at the Swan House."

Ginger hummed. "It seems to be the brothel du jour. Please let me know what you discover."

After ending her call with Magna, Ginger made another call to the operator, asking for Scotland Yard, but unfortunately, Basil wasn't in. In the background, Ginger could hear a loud discussion about a disturbance in Trafalgar Square.

"No," she responded when the officer asked if she wanted to leave a message. "It can wait."

Ginger finished her correspondence, then, with Boss following, his nails tapping on the marble tiles, she found Digby. "Please have someone pop these envelopes in the post," she said. Then, scooping Boss into her arms, she scratched his ears before handing him over to the butler. "Perhaps, if Pippins is free, he wouldn't mind taking Boss for a little jaunt in the back garden."

Digby accepted her pet with a gracious nod. "Indeed, Mr. Pippins was asking after the doggie, Mrs. Reed. I'm certain he'd be delighted."

"I'll be stepping out for a bit," Ginger announced. Digby's eyes widened at the fact that his arms were packed with both Boss and the letters.

"It's all right, Digby," she said with a smile. "I can collect my coat myself."

"Very well, madam," Digby said before heading down the corridor towards the back garden.

Ginger called after him. "Please inform Clement that I'll be taking the Crossley."

HALEY LOVED HER JOB.

Most people felt squeamish around the dead, as if the mere presence of death would cause it to somehow rub off on them. The lifelessness of what had once been a living and breathing complex entity could disconcert those still living. Unseeing eyes that had once been the window of the owner's soul. A soul with hopes and dreams, the ability to both hate and love, and a body that could enjoy the pleasures of romance, food, music, and art.

Haley found solace with the dead because she respected the sanctity of life. She offered them one last moment of dignity. Preparing their body, their earthly vessel, for its final resting place and giving those who loved them, who were left behind, a way forward to grieve and say farewell.

Peace came with the truth, even when the truth was

terrible to hear. How had their loved one died? And at whose hand? Was justice needed? Haley found great fulfilment in knowing that her work sometimes played an important role in bringing such justice to pass.

At the moment, she was sitting at a desk tucked in the corner of the mortuary, filling out paperwork for Dr. Palmer. He worked at his desk in a connecting office, and Haley had a strange sense of relief knowing she was out of sight.

Not because his seeing her displeased her but because it had the opposite effect on her. When he watched her, whether he thought she knew he was doing so or not, butterflies came to life in her stomach, her cheeks grew warm, and she spent far too much time needlessly pushing hair behind her ears. She jumped when a knock sounded on the door.

"Ginger?" Haley said with mild surprise. "Did we make plans to meet today? Forgive me, but I don't remember."

"No, no, and please don't get up," Ginger said. "My calling in is rather impromptu. Are you very busy?"

"Not at all. In fact, I was thinking about taking a coffee break." There was a small coffee and tea counter in the mortuary.

Ginger sat in an empty wooden chair just as Dr. Palmer entered the main room from his office.

"Good afternoon, Mrs. Reed," he said. "I thought I heard voices."

"Good afternoon, Dr. Palmer," Ginger returned. "I hope I'm not interrupting."

"Not at all," the doctor said. "You caught us during a slow bit." He smiled at Haley. "I believe it's time for a coffee break as well. However, I'm afraid I'm needed elsewhere. Miss Higgins, can you manage the mortuary for a while? I shan't be long."

"Certainly, Dr. Palmer." Haley's full lips twitched as she struggled not to smile. She moved her gaze from the doctor to Ginger, whose green eyes sparkled knowingly. Haley sniffed, then busied herself with the coffee-making.

When Dr. Palmer had left, Ginger said lightly, "You two seem to be getting on swimmingly."

"We share similar interests, that's all," Haley said. "I really don't want to become attached, Ginger. I've got my career, and I can't forget about Joe." As much as Haley would have liked to fall in love and pretend everything was coming up roses, the fact remained that her brother's murderer was still at large. Haley could never stay away from Boston in a permanent fashion until his case was solved.

"Very well," Ginger said, accepting her cup of coffee. "I'm not here to discuss your love life or lack thereof."

Haley settled into her chair with her cup of coffee in hand. "What do you want to discuss?"

"Basil's case, of course." Ginger leaned closer. "Have you learned anything new?"

"As a matter of fact, the blood tests came back about half an hour ago. I called Hartigan House, but you'd already left."

Ginger tapped her fingertips on the desktop. "And?"

"Nevomax. You know the one."

"Ah," Ginger said. Nevomax, when injected into the muscle, spreads quickly, targeting nerve cells. The rapid results made it a favoured poison of choice during the Great War. "Do you know how it was administered?"

"It appears to have entered through the marks on the neck. I did a thorough search of Miss Oakley's body, and I didn't find any other puncture marks anywhere. Though alcohol was found in her system, there were no drugs. Just the poison."

"Do you know what was used to make the bite mark?"

Haley shook her head. "No. That's still a mystery. What about you? Do you have a suspect list?"

"Not a good one," Ginger said. "There's Mr. Keene, the museum manager; his secretary, Mr. Lockhart; and the artist Mr. Mathers who worked on the original figurine of the victim."

"And what motives do they have?" Haley asked.

"Well, Mr. Keene denies being a visitor to the Swan House, and if my instincts are right, I'm inclined to believe him."

"What do you mean?"

"Only I got the sense that he and his secretary were more than just employer and employee." For added clarification, she added, "Beyond friend."

"Ah," Haley said with understanding. "And Mr. Mathers?"

Ginger shook her head. "Nothing is jumping out for him so far. Magna's looking into his background, but other than a spot of infidelity, there's no apparent motive to kill."

"I see. Are they the only three?"

"I hate even to say it because the idea is preposterous."

Haley raised a brow with interest. "Who?"

"Alfred Schofield."

Haley couldn't hold in a scoffing chuckle. "How'd he make it onto the list?"

"He also frequents the Swan House, and one of the women there told us—Basil and me—

that Dinah Oakley was his preference."

"So, you and Basil are working the case together?"

"It's complicated. I believe Basil is torn between wanting my help and wanting to protect me. I was there at my own insistence."

Haley laughed. "Basil knows you too well to demand that you keep your nose out of his business."

Ginger huffed. "It's not just his business. It's a matter of crimes against women being taken seriously. If it weren't for the sensationalism of the last victim, I . . ." She waved at Haley. ". . . We probably still wouldn't have heard about it. Those women's deaths didn't even merit making the newspapers!"

Haley shared Ginger's indignation regarding that fact. "I'm sorry for laughing, honey. You're right. This isn't a laughing matter. I'll do what I can to help."

Setting her half-empty cup down on Haley's desk, Ginger stood and smoothed the skirt of her dress. "You are a great help, Haley. I have a few stops to make, and then I'm heading home. Will I see you there?" With a slight smirk, she added, "Or do you have dinner plans with the fine doctor tonight."

"We're dining out tomorrow night." Haley's shoulders straightened. "As colleagues."

It was Ginger's turn to laugh. "If you say so, love. Bye-bye."

Haley watched her friend sashay across the floor as if she were modelling in a fashion show rather than entering an empty mortuary. She and Ginger Reed, formerly Gold, were unlikely friends, but Haley was exceedingly grateful for their friendship.

It was late afternoon with dusk approaching as Ginger drove along the streets of London on her way home. The newer electric street lamps were lighting up, the older gas lamps being attended to by men whose job was to climb ladders and light them. One day the whole city would be lit by electricity, a thought foreign to most people, including Ginger, only a decade earlier. Even so, plenty of stretches of road lacked sufficient light, especially with fog beginning to thicken. Ginger had to use the brake pedal more than she'd like, but at least her Crossley had good headlamps.

Ginger's mind wasn't on the patchy lighting or

growing fogginess. Her mind was on Nevomax. The poison caused a rapid onset of painful and distressing symptoms, starting with heart palpitations, followed by paralysis, and ultimately respiratory failure, bringing death.

The poisoning and death had to have occurred inside or at least out of view of witnesses. This meant the women found in side streets had been moved there after death. Dinah Oakley had been moved after her death.

So where were these women dying? At the brothel? No. The chances of being caught out were too great. The killer must've enticed them to come to his home or another private lodging after dark, so that they wouldn't be seen. This wouldn't be difficult for women such as these, who were used to using discretion.

The method of injection, the two-pronged object, was a mystery. Ginger couldn't imagine such a device—

Her thought was interrupted by a bang and a crash which brought the Crossley to a sudden stop.

"Oh mercy," she said aloud. One headlamp had gone out, and the other shone dimly. Unfortunately, Ginger found herself in a foggy stretch, and the road she'd taken without thinking was particularly dark.

With a sigh, Ginger stepped out of the Crossley. A quick examination confirmed a dented bonnet, the result of encountering a gas streetlight that hadn't been lit.

There was nothing left to do but abandon the motorcar and walk for help. Digging a small torch out of her handbag, she took a shortcut down a lane that would take her to the next busy street where she'd be sure to spot a taxicab and wave it down. With darkness drawing nigh, all good citizens were indoors, and if not, walked in groups of two or more.

Ginger's situation was neither of those. The lane grew darker as she moved away from the lighted street behind her, the shadows cast by the overgrown plane tree looked eerily human. Ginger stilled at what sounded like a snapping twig. She spun to see who was behind her, her pulse jumping at the thought that she was being followed. Her hand moved to her handbag, feeling for the Remington, her chest tightening at the realization that she hadn't thought it necessary to carry it with her.

"Who's there?"

Only the wind answered her, shaking the branches of the plane tree. Ginger let out a breath. It was only her imagination. She picked up her pace, nearly jogging to the light at the end of the lane.

13

In his office at Scotland Yard, Basil shook a newspaper as if the sharp act would knock the blasted words off the page: *The Dracula Killer Strikes Again!* The sensational headline hardly helped his cause, only giving the killer the attention he desired whilst putting the citizens of London on edge—especially those who lived in the poorer areas where unlawful deeds were more common, particularly after dark.

Not only that, Morris was breathing down his neck, threatening a demotion. The superintendent was known for his blusterous outbursts, but one of these days, he might just follow through with his threats.

That was the other thing. Basil had received only

two letters—neither was a warning or a "game piece", at least that Basil could tell. The writer was writing as if they were friends but carefully leaving out identifying markers like names or places.

Pushing the newspaper aside, he stared at the two letters on his desk, reading them for the hundredth time as if *this* time would make a difference and sense would kick in.

The first one, where he'd referred to Jack the Ripper, had made Basil's spine cool as, at that time, they hadn't yet discovered the first victim, had no way to stop the killing, and didn't know what damage the madman would do to the body.

The second letter had come after Miss Oakley was found at Madame Tussaud's wax museum and had emphasised a fictional villain.

Chief Inspector,

Was Dracula really a terrible monster? Or did this attribute belong to his creator, Mr. Stoker? Perhaps the two were one and the same, and neither could help themselves. I'm rather like our Whitechapel fellow, under a spell and fascinated by blood. You must know the type.

D

At the very least, it was a confession of compulsion. Basil believed the killer knew he'd never stop, which was why he was taunting the police. He wanted to be caught.

There was a tap at the door, and the desk officer entered with a small piece of paper in hand. "Oh, Chief Inspector," he said, "I didn't realise you were here. Your missus rang for you." He placed the note on Basil's desk, and Basil could see the scribble stating Ginger had called for him.

"Did she leave a message?" Basil asked.

"No, sir."

Basil fought back the growing nervousness in his belly. He didn't mind Ginger ringing him at the Yard, but he minded when she didn't leave a message. Her reason for ringing was probably benign, but one could never know. His mind went to little Rosa. Ginger would have asked him to return quickly to Hartigan House if something was the matter with his daughter.

Using the older-style candlestick telephone, Basil rang the operator and gave her the number for Hartigan House. Digby came on the line and told him the disappointing news that Ginger had left the premises and hadn't said where she was going. His next calls were to Feathers & Flair and Ginger's investigation office. Ginger hadn't been to her shop yet that day, and there wasn't anyone at the office to answer the telephone.

Basil exhaled as he hung the black cone-shaped receiver back on its bracket on the boxy wooden telephone secured to the wall. Whatever Ginger had to tell him was not important and could wait until they were alone together, sharing a brandy in the sitting room.

He'd only just returned to his office when the same officer came in behind him, breathless this time.

"Sir, there's another body."

Basil stiffened. "Female? Same modus operandi?"

"That's what the caller said, sir."

"Where?"

"In the lane behind the Swan House. There are a couple of bobbies on site."

Basil grabbed his coat and shrugged it on. "Braxton!"

His constable appeared. "I heard, sir," he said, fastening on his helmet. "Shall I drive?"

They took one of the police motorcars, and Basil took the passenger seat. He could think more clearly if he didn't have to worry about dodging erratic motorcar drivers who barely knew how to operate their machines, or slow-moving horse-drawn wagons and carriages.

"This is number five, isn't it?" Braxton said with a shake of his head.

"I'm afraid so. This case has got me flummoxed, Braxton. Five women dead, and I've got no clear leads."

"It's a puzzle, sir."

Basil huffed. A puzzle had an answer, one clue leading the way to the next. "How was the victim discovered?" he asked.

"Apparently, a barking dog wouldn't let up. When someone went to shoo it away, they saw the woman lying there. At first, it wasn't clear she was dead, but then he saw"—Braxton placed two fingers on his neck—"the marks."

It was a bumpy ride along the cobblestones, and Basil held a palm against the dash. Braxton brought the police vehicle to a stop but left the headlamps pointed at the bobbies who stood by the body.

The light of the headlamps fanned out, dissipating the further it reached. Basil could make out the woman lying on her back, the blue of her coat standing out in the light.

Basil's heart skipped. The coat. He recognised it. Made of wool dyed a brilliant royal blue, the coat had a light grey fur collar. It was one of Ginger's favourites.

"No!"

Basil jumped out of the police vehicle and ran, his chest so tight he could barely breathe. *Ginger.*

Holding his breath, Basil pinched his eyes shut. It was Ginger's coat, but it wasn't Ginger. It was Annie Camden lying there, eyes unseeing. He then remembered that Ginger had given this poor woman her coat.

"Are you all right, sir?"

Basil snapped to reality at the sound of Braxton's voice. "Yes, yes. I am. Let's take a closer look, shall we?"

The still female lying on her back had her eyes wide open, and her chin pushed out, exposing the two red dots on her neck.

"Officers have combed the area but found nothing of note," Braxton offered.

Basil spoke to the attending bobbies. "I'm assuming the doctor has been summoned."

The nearest one adjusted his chinstrap. "Yes, sir. In fact," he pointed in the direction beyond Basil's shoulder, "that's him now."

Basil pivoted on his heel as Palmer approached. "Another Dracula victim?" the doctor said.

"You've been reading the newspapers." Basil disliked the moniker, but the doctor wasn't wrong.

Palmer set his black bag on the ground by his feet, tugged on his trousers, and squatted. "So young," he said. "Such a shame." With his gloved hand, he moved Annie Camden's chin. "Same method. My guess is the killer used Nevomax again."

"Again?" Basil asked.

"The laboratory tests on the blood came in just recently. I'm certain Miss Higgins has let the Met know, but I'll make sure when I return to the hospital."

"What is Nevomax?" Basil asked. "I don't recall hearing about it."

"It's not as common as strychnine or arsenic."

Basil inclined his head in interest. "Is it difficult to come by?"

"It's hard to say," Palmer replied. "It's probably available on the black market." The doctor made a few more rudimentary checks on the body. "Doesn't appear to have any broken bones, but I'll be able to register any contusions once her garments are no longer an impediment."

The reports Basil had read on the previous

victims were much the same—no broken bones or new bruising. One could assume the women were following through on the killer's fantasy, unaware of his devious plan, and had succumbed to the poisonous "bite" on their neck. "Any idea how the poison was administered?" he asked.

Palmer stood. "Believe it or not, it was from the puncture wounds on the neck. I'm afraid I can't tell you much beyond that."

Once the ambulance arrived, Basil watched the body be transported away. Palmer picked up his black bag. "I'll let you know if I discover anything new, Chief Inspector."

"That would be appreciated," Basil said as they walked away. "Oh, and would you mind doing me a favour? Take extra care with Miss Camden's coat." Everything Annie Camden was wearing, including any jewellery and hairpins, would be put in a bag as evidence for the police.

It was late when Basil got back to Hartigan House. He was pleased to find Ginger waiting for him in the sitting room.

"We've both had a long day, love," she said. She poured two fingers of brandy into a glass and handed it to him. Her startling green eyes flashed with regret. "I crashed the Crossley. Gave myself a little fright, but I took a taxicab to the nearest garage and arranged for them to collect my motorcar. The nice fellow gave me a lift home."

Basil pulled his wife into a firm embrace and kissed her deeply.

"Oh mercy," Ginger said with a giggle. "What was that for?"

"For staying alive, love," Basil said. "For staying with me and staying alive."

14

The next morning, a messenger arrived at Hartigan House with a large yellow manila envelope addressed to Ginger. The blocky initials—M.J.—on the top left corner left no doubt that the contents inside had been sent by Magna. Ginger opened the packet in the privacy of her study, dumping a pile of photographs on her desk. Sighing, she arranged the images in order, the target in question being Alfred Schofield. If one held the photographs in a stack and flipped the edges, one could nearly see the action play out, much like with a cartoon flip book. Alfred approaching Annie Camden, the two conferring, Alfred peering over his shoulder, Alfred following Annie, Alfred entering the Swan House.

Things definitely didn't look good for Alfred.

A while later the police arrived to take Alfred in for questioning. Mrs. Schofield was in an uproar. In an uncharacteristic manner, instead of sending a message with her maid, Ginger's elderly neighbour pounded on the front door of Hartigan House with her cane.

"Mrs. Reed! Mr. Reed!"

Her brittle, aged voice echoed through the entrance hall when Digby opened the door. "There's been a terrible mistake," Mrs. Schofield screeched. "They've taken Alfred!"

"Please come in, Mrs. Schofield," Ginger said as she ushered her in. "Digby, arrange for tea in the sitting room."

Ambrosia had heard the commotion, which was difficult not to hear—the way sound bounced about the high ceilings and along the corridor of the second level of the house. By the time the dowager Lady Gold had joined them, the knocking of her walking stick on the marble tile announcing her approach, Mrs. Schofield had calmed her hysterics and was left to sniffing loudly into her lace-trimmed handkerchief.

Guiding Mrs. Schofield by her elbow, Ginger led the distraught lady to the sitting room and assisted her into one of the lemon-tinted-velvet wingback chairs. The sitting room was a favourite of Ginger's with its Persian carpet, tall windows that let in natural light, and rugged stone fireplace, currently lit with warmth from the red coals.

Ginger's maid Lizzie had been tasked with bringing in the tea trolley. Ginger liked Lizzie best as she had been with her the longest and, in Ginger's opinion, had the most appealing disposition.

Seeing the state of poor Mrs. Schofield and how Ginger was administering comforting pats on her shoulder, Lizzie asked, "Shall I pour, madam?" Though the task would normally go to Ambrosia, her hands had begun to shake of late, and an unspoken understanding had been reached between them.

"Yes, please," Ginger said.

Sitting upright as one who still insisted on wearing a Victorian corset must, Ambrosia cleared her throat. "Will someone tell me what disaster has come upon us?"

Mrs. Schofield looked up from her handkerchief with glassy, bloodshot eyes. "They've taken my Alfred."

After accepting a cup of tea from Lizzie, Ambrosia asked, "Who's taken him?"

Mrs. Schofield blew on her tea. "The police."

Ambrosia sniffed. "Whatever for?"

Mrs. Schofield blushed with mortification, but she sipped her tea instead of answering.

Of course Ginger already knew the answer. They didn't have direct proof that Alfred had been responsible for Annie Camden's death, but Magna's photographs of him with Annie were damning.

"Mrs. Schofield," Ambrosia started. "Must you persist in keeping us in suspense?"

"I'm so very sorry," Mrs. Schofield choked out. "It's just so very dreadful."

Ginger took Mrs. Schofield's hand as she answered Ambrosia on Mrs. Schofield's behalf. "I know from Basil that Alfred is a potential witness to a crime that occurred last night. I'm sure that's all it is," Ginger said kindly. She certainly hoped that was the case. "The police only need to question him."

"But they were so unkind and impatient. The whole street watched as the officers manhandled my Alfred and pushed him into the backseat of the motorcar."

"That doesn't sound like simply questioning," Ambrosia said.

Ginger shot her a look. "We mustn't jump to conclusions."

"What kind of crime is he accused of?" Ambrosia asked.

Mrs. Schofield's eyes darted to Ginger before she again broke into tears.

"Oh, for goodness' sake. It had better be a murder with this performance."

Mrs. Schofield sobbed. "It *is* murder, Lady Gold. Involving those . . . *those* . . . women!"

Ambrosia's round eyes drilled into Ginger. "The women of the night killings?"

"Yes, Grandmother," Ginger answered coolly, "And please don't dismiss it as inconsequential because of your bias."

"Nonsense," Ambrosia blustered. "This is just evidence of where such immoral and licentious living leads. But I don't wish anyone dead, Ginger. I'm not a monster."

Ginger sipped her tea, thankful that Mrs. Schofield had calmed herself.

"What do you know about this?" Ambrosia said. "With your connections. Surely Basil and Miss Higgins can shed some light."

"All I know is that the women are being poisoned," Ginger said. "Unfortunately, the killer is very good at covering his steps and hasn't left a clear clue behind."

Mrs. Schofield sniffed and lifted her chin. "Well, I can tell you that my Alfred had nothing to do with such salacious activities. He's had a hard go of it since the war, but he's a good boy."

After a cup of tea, Mrs. Schofield was calm enough to be escorted home by Clement. She'd only been gone a few minutes when the front door chime was heard.

Ambrosia leaned on her walking stick. "It's like Piccadilly Circus around here."

However, the elderly Lady Gold's mood quickly changed when Digby opened the sitting room door and produced Felicia. After losing her husband, the dowager had brought up her grandchildren the best she could after her son and daughter-in-law were killed in a carriage crash. She always said Daniel had been a delight, whilst Felicia, several years Daniel's junior, had been a wild horse.

Ginger jumped to her feet. "Felicia! You're back!"

Felicia's youthful grey eyes sparkled with delight as she looked at everyone in the room. She warmly embraced Ginger and Ambrosia before sitting on the settee beside her grandmother.

"I thought you and Charles were returning next month," Ambrosia said. "It's rather inconsiderate to change one's plans without notifying those waiting for you."

"Oh, Grandmama!" Felicia smiled as she patted her perfectly coiffed brunette bob. "I wanted to surprise you. And look, I have!"

"Indeed," Ginger said. "Shall I ring for a fresh pot of tea?"

"If you don't feel like you're about to float away from consuming too much already," Felicia said. Eyeing the third abandoned teacup, she added, "Who did I miss?"

Ginger rang the bell for the kitchen. "Mrs. Schofield. I'm afraid she's had a shock. But before we extend our gossip to you, you must tell us about your trip."

Felicia crossed her legs, knee over knee, and bounced her foot—a carefree display that Ambrosia had often scolded her for as the "behaviour of unsavoury women." Now that Felicia was married, and to an earl at that, Ambrosia had learned to keep her tongue, but the tension around her eyes and mouth betrayed her displeasure.

"We had a fabulous time in Edinburgh. Charles had many meetings there, so I had time to shop untethered!" Jumping to her feet, she twirled, displaying a new floral-print day frock with flouncy tiers in the skirt and the wide sash tied into a large, loose bow at the base of the lower back. A short string of pearls sat long on her delicate collarbones, accenting the swooped neckline. "And this"—she pointed to a rectangular leather bag with straps on the short end—"is my prized buy." She unbuckled the top flap and slipped out a camera. "It's a Voigtländer Bergheil, the latest model."

With what was clearly a newly learned finesse, Felicia expanded the accordion-style face of the camera, held the contraption to her face, and pretended to snap. "It's been terribly exciting shooting the great castles in the area. Edinburgh Castle was lovely, but I preferred the unnerving ruins of Slains Castle. When Charles had some time off, we hired a motorcar and drove north along the craggy coastline to see it." She fell back into her chair and proclaimed, "It was smashing!"

"Speaking of Slains Castle," Ginger started. "Madame Tussaud's wax museum opened whilst you were away."

Lizzie entered with a tray holding a fresh pot of tea, a clean cup for Felicia, and a plate of ginger biscuits.

As Ginger served everyone, Felicia asked, "Did you go? Wait, is there a Dracula exhibit?"

Ginger settled back in her armchair. After a sip of tea, she explained how the fourth of five bodies had been positioned there and the strange method of killing.

"A nod to Bram Stoker, surely," Felicia said. "How clever of Haley to notice. But what does that have to do with Mrs. Schofield?"

"All the victims are prostitutes from a brothel in Villiers Street," Ginger said, ignoring the tense expression that formed on Ambrosia's face at the word "prostitute"."Alfred's return to London coincides with the timing of the killings, and unfortunately, he's a frequent visitor to the brothel in question."

"As distasteful as that is, I'm sure he can't be the only man keeping the brothel in business," Felicia noted.

"That's true," Ginger said, "but he was recently seen with two of the victims."

Felicia pouted her lips. "Oh dear."

Ginger wondered if Felicia remembered her first meeting with Alfred Schofield. She had behaved like an uninhibited "bright young thing" and had flirted shamelessly with the man. Ginger was pleased to see how her former sister-in-law had matured over the last few years. The Earl of Witt, now Felicia's husband, had been a good influence on her.

"Well, I do hope he's not the killer," Felicia said.

"Indeed," Ambrosia blustered. "Can you imagine living next door to a mass murderer? We'd never live it down."

Ginger was about to object to the sentiment; however, Ambrosia's self-interest was too common to comment on.

Digby entered. "Mrs. Reed, a telephone call came in for you. Mr. Reed left a message asking if you could come to Scotland Yard as soon as it suited you." He handed her a note that she found intriguing.

Mr. Alfred Schofield refuses to speak to anyone but Mrs. Reed.

"Scotland Yard needs you, Ginger," Felicia said with a smile. "Some things never change."

Ginger smoothed out her frock as she got to her feet. "Thank you, Digby," she said, adding, "Drat, my Crossley is still at the garage."

"What happened to your Crossley?" Felicia asked with a grin. "Did you finally crash into a lamp post?"

Ginger eyed Felicia but didn't think her lucky guess justified a response. "Digby, please ring for a taxicab. Felicia, shall we go out for lunch tomorrow?"

"I'd love that. I'll drive."

Charles had bought Felicia a new Mercedes-Benz. And since Ginger's own Crossley was still in the garage, she agreed. "See you then."

15

*G*inger put on a simple, sophisticated Coco Chanel light grey day frock with a wide-pleated skirt to prepare for her encounter with Alfred Schofield. A black belt was tied loosely at the hips. She added a multi-rope of pearls, pearl earrings, and a black felt hat with a short brim.

As she dressed, her mind worked the case. Things didn't look good for Alfred. A man given over to drugs and other "weaknesses of the flesh" could find himself doing something terrible. Something he'd never dreamed of doing when his mind and body were stronger. Had his masculinity been ridiculed? Had he suffered too many romantic rejections? Could her neighbour have harboured an inner monster waiting for the right trigger to unleash it?

And why had he insisted on speaking only to her?

There was only one way to find out.

The taxicab was waiting at the kerb in front of Hartigan House when Ginger walked out of the entrance and down the cement pathway to the short iron fence that encased the front garden. The gate opened smoothly as Clement tended to the hinges regularly.

The driver took the route through Belgravia and along the delightful park-like Eaton Square, which reminded Ginger of another murder case in one of the grander London houses. Soon the taxicab was in Westminster, motoring past the iconic Westminster Abbey and the towering Big Ben clock until they reached Scotland Yard on Victoria Embankment, just down the road.

Scotland Yard operated out of two four-storey Victorian-style buildings constructed with red brick and accentuated with bands of white Portland stone.

Loud voices reached her as she stepped into the ground-level reception area; Ginger entered a commotion that was well underway. Two women wore police-like uniforms—skirts rather than trousers, low-heeled leather boots, masculine-style black ties knotted at the collars of starchy white blouses, and on their heads, particularly unappealing dark hats with unfashionably wide brims. They had stern expressions of self-righteousness, staring with disapproval at another younger woman whom Ginger recognised. Helen Forbes glared back at them with fury.

"These women think they are above the rest of us!" Miss Forbes' face was flushed a deep red.

"We are members of the Metropolitan Police Women Patrols," the stouter woman replied. "As such, we have the authority to bring wayward women to the attention of the police."

"I'm hardly a wayward woman!" Miss Forbes' face flushed with crimson indignation. "And even if I were, I'm a free citizen of Britain, and as such, I have the right to travel across the city as I wish."

Seeing Ginger, Miss Forbes reached for her arm as if grasping a lifeline. "Mrs. Reed, I was merely taking a shortcut home when these two, for no reason, demanded I accompany them here. They enlisted the aid of a passing bobby, so I was helpless to deny them."

"Miss Forbes was unaccompanied in a questionable part of the city," the leader said. Lowering her voice, she added, "Near that den of iniquity called the Swan House. Ne'er-do-wells loiter about that area with nefarious intentions to recruit naive young women into a lifestyle of vice."

As if to support her colleague's position, the stout one quickly added, "One must simply attend a rally led by Gerald Hall. He's the man of the hour, mark my words. He supports the work we do."

"Mr. Hall is a snake," Miss Forbes said venomously. "I'm an educated woman, not a naive girl. I live on my own and can take care of myself."

"Be that as it may," the stout one said. "Young female minds are gullible."

Ginger tensed with indignation. "I can vouch for Miss Forbes. She is in no danger of being swept away by devious men. Would you release her to me if I commit to taking full responsibility for her welfare and ensuring she gets home safely?"

The two women sniffed as they shared looks of discontent. Ginger's position as a chief inspector's wife was well known among the police, and as she had anticipated, the women relented. "Very well, Mrs. Reed," the tall one said. "Good day, then."

The policewomen marched out, and Ginger hoped they'd find more to do with their time than to terrorise young women. "Miss Forbes?" she said. Helen Forbes smoothed out her tartan coat and adjusted her cloche hat, forcing a controlled breath as she did so.

"Thank you, Mrs. Reed. We females have enough disparity to deal with when it comes to the men in our company that it's simply disheartening that other women oppose us as well."

Ginger had to agree. "I'm afraid I can't accompany you home now as I promised. Would you be willing to wait for me?"

"I'm quite capable of finding my own way home," Miss Forbes said. "It's the middle of the day. It's not like I'll be ambushed in the middle of the street."

"Very well," Ginger said. "Do take care, and perhaps refrain from taking shortcuts through Soho, at least on your own. It wouldn't do for you to be apprehended again."

Miss Forbes turned with a huff. "I shouldn't be apprehended at all."

Ginger agreed with the feisty young woman and understood the frustration of being ahead of the times.

. . .

GINGER RECALLED the first time she'd met Alfred Schofield, shortly after moving back to London. Then, he was a dashing, upright citizen who strutted about confidently as one with the world at his feet. Now, sitting in the interrogation room, he looked defeated. His shoulders sloped forward, his hair was unkempt, his eyes were bloodshot with dark rings around them, and he had the sallow skin of one who seemed not to have slept in days.

He smoked a cigarette, tapping ash into an ashtray with a shaky hand. When he saw Ginger through the window, he straightened as if a change in posture could hide his sorry state.

"Lady Gold," he said as Basil ushered her in. "So good of you to come."

"It's my pleasure," Ginger said as she sat beside Basil on the opposite side of the table from Alfred. "I'm told you're refusing to speak to anyone else."

Alfred darted a look of contempt in Basil's direction, then said, "I don't trust the police."

"But you trust me?" Ginger returned. "I'm married to a policeman."

"You have a foot in both worlds, Mrs. Reed," Alfred said. "You understand how they work without being one of them. I need a savvy advocate." He stabbed the ashtray with his half-smoked cigarette. "I don't want to hang for a crime I didn't commit."

"Perhaps you should engage a solicitor." Ginger stared at Alfred pointedly.

Basil replied for the man. "Mr. Fossey is on his way."

"Shall we wait for him?" Ginger asked, but a knock on the door soon presented Mr. Fossey, who had an air of overworked agitation. He sat beside Alfred, setting his briefcase and hat on his lap, then said, "My client wishes to cooperate but will not respond to questions that may incriminate him."

"I want to clear my name and go home." The words coming out of Alfred's mouth sounded youthful, and Ginger had a flash image of what Alfred would've been like as a boy when suffering from childish regret.

"Then let's proceed," Ginger said. "Were you at the Swan House last night?"

Alfred shifted in his chair, his gaze wandering to the ceiling. Ginger continued, "I'm a mature lady of the world, Mr. Schofield. Nothing you say will shock me. I'm not here to judge you. Simply to uncover the truth."

Mr. Fossey whispered in Alfred's ear. Alfred relented. "Yes, I was there."

"Were you with Miss Camden?" Ginger asked.

After a nod from Mr. Fossey, Alfred said, "You mean Annie? Yes, but she was alive when I left her. I swear!"

Basil interjected. "What time would that be?"

When another nod came from the solicitor, Alfred said, "I'm not absolutely certain. Before dawn."

"Were you not wearing your wristwatch?" Ginger asked.

Alfred raised his left arm, revealing a bare wrist. "It's broken."

"How did it break?" Basil asked.

Ginger cast him a glance. Had Alfred broken his timepiece whilst wrestling Miss Camden into submission or disposing of the body?

"It fell off my bedside table," Alfred said, missing the shaking of his solicitor's head. "And I accidentally stepped on it."

"How often did you visit the Swan House?" Ginger asked. When Alfred raised a brow, she clarified, "We know you liked to visit Miss Oakley."

"Don't answer that," Mr. Fossey said. "My client's whereabouts are circumstantial at best. Plenty of other men are also culpable if visiting *these* women is the requirement for detainment. I demand you release my client immediately and cease this harassment."

To Ginger's surprise, Basil removed a paper evidence bag from his pocket and held it upside down. A man's wristwatch with a broken glass face. "Do you recognise this watch?" Basil asked.

The despairing look on Alfred's face was all the answer Ginger needed.

"This was found in Miss Camden's boudoir," Basil said. "Mr. Fossey, I'm afraid we'll be retaining your client for a while longer."

"But—" Alfred began, but Mr. Fossey raised a palm.

"Don't speak, Mr. Schofield. Anything can and shall be used against you in a court of law."

Alfred was taken back to the cells as his stern-faced solicitor, briefcase in hand, marched away.

Ginger turned to Basil. "You never mentioned Alfred's wristwatch had been found."

"It was only retrieved this morning, love, and we didn't know who it belonged to. I'm actually surprised Alfred showed his hand so quickly."

"I think he was rather stunned. And sleep deprived. The poor man looks dreadful."

"He's only going to feel worse, I'm afraid," Basil

said. "The Met doesn't provide cocaine to its inmates."

Ginger grimaced. "Alfred won't be the first to feel the effects of a distasteful withdrawal."

Basil instructed a constable to ring for a taxicab for Ginger. "Will you be heading home, love?" he asked.

"I'll drop in at the shop on my way," Ginger said. "We're quite busy preparing for the spring fashion line. You wouldn't believe the orders that have come in already. Dear Emma is working the Singer machine to death."

Basil held the door open for Ginger when the taxicab arrived, kissing her cheek before she got in. Ginger gave the driver the address of her Regent Street shop, then, as an afterthought, said, "Actually, can you take me to the office of Mr. Gerald Hall instead?"

GINGER WAITED until Gerald Hall's receptionist was distracted, which happened with the convenient arrival of the postman. She quickly stepped past the receptionist and hurried to Mr. Hall's cracked-open office door. Looking inside, Ginger could see the impressively large, furnished room with a large, stylish desk and inviting plush chairs.

"Madam!"

The receptionist, now seeing Ginger, walked briskly towards her like a schoolmarm about to hand out a scolding. "Mr. Hall's diary today is quite full. If you come with me, I will gladly make you an appointment to see him."

Ginger glanced back through the crack; the receptionist's commotion having caught Mr. Hall's attention. When he spotted Ginger, he got to his feet and came to the door.

"It's quite all right, Miss Wells," he said with his trademark, overly wide smile. "I always have time for a beautiful young lady. Mrs. Reed. What a pleasant surprise."

Ginger held in her mild surprise that he knew her name. But then again, she had gained some publicity as a businesswoman and the wife of a chief inspector. Her family was no stranger to the society pages of the London newspapers.

Mr. Hall waved Ginger inside his office. "Do come in."

"Thank you for seeing me without an appointment," Ginger said as she stepped past the man. "I'll be brief."

Mr. Hall's lips turned into what Ginger could only call a smarmy smile. "I've got all the time in the world for a pretty lady like you." He waved to the empty one sitting in front of the desk, he said, "Have a seat."

Ginger almost declined, but it didn't help her cause to put the man in a defensive position. Mr. Hall tugged on the legs of his expensive pinstripe suit trousers before sitting in his desk chair.

"I'm coming to you as a concerned citizen," Ginger started. "Are you aware of the trouble on Villiers Street?"

Mr. Hall tsked, his cheeks bulging as he pulled in his lips. He shook his head with displeasure. "A deuced shame, Mrs. Reed. Forgive my harsh language, but the immorality has gone on for too long. As a councillor, I promise to do my utmost to clear those women out."

"Where will you 'clear them out' to?"

The politician jerked. "What do you mean?"

"Surely the question must've come up before now. What will happen to the women when you 'clear them out'?"

Mr. Hall's mouth curled into a stiff smile. "Well, you don't have to worry your pretty little head about that, Mrs. Reed. The problem will be taken care of.

You can go on with your tea parties and shopping sprees without concern."

Ginger bristled at the man's patronising tone. "I am concerned, Mr. Hall, about these women. Perhaps a more compassionate stance is in order. You must be aware that it's poverty resulting from poor wages and not poor moral character on its own that drives these women to do what they do?"

"Ah," Mr. Hall said as he leaned back in his chair and tented his fingers. "You're one of *them*."

"One of whom?"

"The 'Share the Burden' types. Believe me, if these promiscuous women weren't parading their wares about, young men wouldn't fall into temptation."

"Mr. Hall, are you aware that women from Villiers Street are being murdered? There are five victims now."

"Of course I'm aware. That doesn't happen to wholesome women who know their place in society. Good wives and mothers are what we need." Mr. Hall got to his feet. "Now, if there's nothing else, I'm a very busy man."

Ginger stood, shooting the man a piercing glare. "I'm certain you are, Mr. Hall. Thank you for this very enlightening conversation. Good day."

Mr. Hall called after her as she headed for the door. "Can I count on your vote?"

Pretending not to hear him, Ginger walked into the corridor as she muttered under her breath, "Over my dead body."

16

*H*aley never intended to get emotionally attached to anyone of the opposite sex while completing her internship in London. She prided herself on keeping a steady, unflappable demeanour that served her well in life, growing up as a tomboy with older brothers and later entering a field known for its attachment to trauma and tragedy.

Not to mention a field dominated by men. Haley had learned to ignore the snide remarks, cruel jesting, and looks of disdain. Being tall worked in her favour as no man liked to stare a woman in the eyes if they were level with his own.

Dr. Neville Palmer had been indifferent towards her on first meeting, but Haley saw this as merely initial shyness. He'd been supportive and helpful, and she'd learned much under his tutelage. She was surprised when he'd asked her out to dinner, and he seemed surprised when the words came out of his mouth.

The Atlantic Ocean was still separating London from Boston, where her heart still lived, but that was a problem for another day. Unlike some women she'd met in the past, Haley could enjoy dinner with a friendly colleague without planning a wedding in the back of her mind.

Dinner that evening was at an Italian restaurant, a rarity in London. It made the Quo Vadis a popular destination for Londoners who wanted an evening that would whisk them away to the Continent for a few hours. It was elegantly designed with high ceilings, ornate chandeliers, framed oil paintings of Rome, and murals of Italian life hanging generously on the walls.

"This makes me miss Boston even more," Haley said. "Boston has a large Italian population, and the food is fantastic."

"My word," Dr. Palmer said, "that's not the outcome I was looking for."

Haley pushed a stubborn curl behind her ear. Ginger had helped her dress for the event, choosing a pink satin gown that Haley would never have chosen for herself. It had an ornate, deep V-neck with an equally deep V down the back. The skirt had a flouncy, uneven hemline with more fabric falling from the sides than the front and back, and the matching belt resting low on the hips had a prominent flashy bauble that looked like a real gem. And Lizzie had performed miracles on her long hair, securing it into a faux bob. But no number of pins could tame every curl. Other women bravely cut their long hair off at the ears, but Haley knew her unruly hair would spring out like an overused broom. Long hair was easier to manage. A ponytail or long braid was pinned up at the back of her neck, keeping her hair out of things like a Bunsen burner flame or away from the edge of a scalpel.

Haley felt somewhat fraudulent and nervously shy arriving in such a flashy ensemble. Still, Ginger had been right, as she usually was regarding fashion, and Dr. Palmer's moment of speechlessness when he first saw her was proof of that.

"You look . . . extravagant," he said. He pulled out a chair for Haley at the table for two he'd reserved, and she tried to make herself comfortable.

Dr. Palmer picked up a menu. "What would you

like to eat? Pasta? Pizza? Oh, and they have seafood as well."

"I'd love a traditional plate of spaghetti," Haley said, though a glance at her borrowed gown caused her to change her mind. She'd get sauce on it unless she was ready to wear the linen napkin as a bib, which she was not. "On second thought, I'll have the baked cod."

The food was ordered, and a bottle of wine arrived. Haley took a sip and wondered if Dr. Palmer was as nervous as she was as he played distractedly with a decorative ring he wore on his thumb. It was in the haematite intaglio style with the profile of an ancient warrior engraved in pewter and embedded on a wide, ornate gold band. Haley noted it only because she'd never seen him wearing it before. Jewellery was an unnecessary and cumbersome accessory in the mortuary.

"I've always been curious about America," he said. "And now, seeing how much you love Boston, I'm interested in visiting someday. I'd like to see what all the fuss is about."

"Boston has a very English feel about it, Dr. Palmer. The area is called New England, but it has a European flair as it's been settled chiefly by the Italians, Germans, Irish, and Jews. Along with the British, of course."

"Not so unlike London," Dr. Palmer said. "I'm surprised at all the ethnicities represented here."

"You've not lived in London long?" Haley asked.

"Only a few months. I'm from Rugeley, just north of Birmingham, where I attended university."

The waiter arrived with Haley's baked cod and pepperoni pizza for Dr. Palmer. Haley was used to eating meals without wine in America's prohibition and found her glass of French merlot wonderfully delightful and guilt-free.

As if he were suddenly uneasy, Dr. Palmer shifted in his seat. "Why did you decide to go into medicine? I mean, it's not something you see many women do."

"I've always been fascinated with science," Haley said. "Facts and figures. I grew up on a farm, so I first thought I'd become a veterinarian."

Dr. Palmer's lips pulled up crookedly. "Most women dream about getting married and having children."

"Well, the Great War upset the man-to-woman ratio, so I figure it's a good thing there are women like me who are interested in other things."

"I find it fascinating that women like yourself

who desire to be treated equally with men still insist on chivalry. They expect men to bring flowers, open doors, pay for dinner."

"Inequality between the sexes is clear. It's only fair that the man makes the token gestures. Even then, the scale remains wildly out of balance."

The corner of Dr. Palmer's eye twitched, and he sipped his wine which seemed to settle it. Haley took advantage of the pause in the conversation to take a bite of cod, which, she'd be happy to report when asked by Ginger, was moist and delicious with a lemon and basil sauce.

Unsurprisingly, talk turned to the current, shocking case, as it was an intriguing topic for both of them.

"I hope the police are well on their way to finding the culprit," Haley said. "Five dead women are five too many."

"Jack the Ripper had at least five," Dr. Palmer said. "And as we all know too well, 'Jack' has yet to be caught."

"It's a shame so many villains get away with their crimes," Haley said, pausing. Should she tell Dr. Palmer about her brother? She normally never talked about what had happened to Joe except with close friends like Ginger. Still, there was something about Dr. Palmer, maybe how the glow of the candlelight softened his features, or maybe it was the calming effects of the wine, but she brought him into her confidence.

"My brother Joe was murdered; his killer is still unknown."

Dr. Palmer's eyes flashed interest, before washing with compassion. He reached across the table to touch her hand. "That must feel terrible."

"It does. This is why this killer must be found and stopped."

"I'm sure Scotland Yard is doing its best," Dr. Palmer said sympathetically. "Police work has improved immensely over the years."

"I suppose," Haley said. However, none of the advancements had brought justice for her brother. She forced a smiled, ready to change the subject. "I hear the tiramisu is very good."

17

"*T*he arrogance of the man!" Ginger relayed the story of her encounter with Gerald Hall over breakfast the next morning. She'd have held her tongue if Ambrosia had been present, but she didn't hold back her distaste with only Basil and Haley as company. "He's a condescending misogynist, and I wouldn't hesitate to put him on the list if there was even one little piece of evidence against him."

Basil raised a dark brow. "The list?"

"The prime suspect list," Ginger said. "I know poor Alfred is at the top, but my gut tells me he's not our man."

This time Basil smiled. "Your gut."

Haley chimed in. "Maybe if you put a piece of toast in your gut, it would keep its nose out of police business."

Ginger persisted. "Alfred is weak and hapless, prone to giving in to sins of the flesh, but he's only out to hurt himself, not others."

"I wish I could be as confident, love." Basil reached for his buttered toast. "Murderers come in all shapes and sizes."

"Besides Alfred Schofield," Haley started, "and the terrible Mr. Hall, is there anyone else who could be culpable?"

Basil sighed. "Our killer is capable, confident, and intelligent. He'd have to be to get away with something like this for this long."

"Or she," Haley said. "Men often underestimate an intelligent woman driven by rage or scorn."

"If the bodies hadn't been moved," Basil said, "I would agree with you, but we're not even finding drag marks or wheel tracks. Whoever is moving dead weight has physical strength."

"Would you categorise Mr. Keene, Mr. Lockhart, or Mr. Mathers as capable, confident, and intelligent?"

"Perhaps not at first glance," Basil said. "But wily folk can be good actors. It's also possible two or three of them worked together. My men are trying to gather evidence to support that theory." Finishing his cup of tea, he pushed away from the table. "And with that, I must excuse myself and depart for the Yard." He kissed Ginger on the cheek and offered Haley wishes for a good day. Turning back to Ginger, he said with amusement flashing in his hazel eyes, "Do try to keep out of trouble, love."

"Of course, darling," Ginger returned. Noting Haley staring with interest, she said, "What is it?"

"Nothing. Just you two seem to be very happy."

Ginger smiled warmly. "We are. I can't believe how fortunate I have been since we journeyed here together on the SS *Rosa*. I never thought I'd marry again, much less have a family." She reached for Haley's arm. "And what about you? How was your date with the handsome doctor?"

Haley offered a soft shrug. "It was pleasant. We make easy conversation since we are interested in many of the same things."

Ginger pouted in response. "That sounds very clinical and not at all romantic."

"We haven't crossed the line into romance, Ginger, and I'm not sure we should." Haley sighed. "I mean, I am attracted to him, but I'm not sure if it's as a man or simply as a doctor I admire. At any rate, he asked me out again."

"Did you say yes?"

"It seemed rude to say no," Haley replied.

Ginger sipped her tea. She'd have liked nothing better than for Haley to be as happy with someone as she herself was with Basil.

After spending an hour with baby Rosa, Ginger headed to her office, where her accounting sat on the desk.

It was uncommon for a woman to run her own business, much less two, and for that, she had her father to thank. He'd had the foresight to ensure she had access to the family bank accounts and had set up a couple extra for her use before he died. Times might have been modern for women in some ways, but not regarding things like voting or finances. Ginger pushed back the simmering rage of injustice, wondering if the day would come when a woman could walk into a bank and open her own bank account or get a loan without needing a man's signature.

Her father had understood the realities of society even if he disagreed with them. He had gone out of his way to tell Ginger and her sister Louisa that they were as intelligent and capable as any man. Her eyes rested on the painted portrait of a younger George Hartigan hanging on the wall, and her heart swelled with emotion. Oh, how she missed him! The study was the only room in the house Ginger hadn't redecorated. This had been her father's study, and she never wanted to erase the memory of him. The colours were still a rich burgundy, the shelves filled with his business manuals, and she could imagine the soft scent of his pipe smoke clinging to the heavy drapery. The room had a way of stirring both comfort and melancholy.

Ginger called to her pet who was curled up on the little dog bed by the fireplace. "Bossy." She patted her lap. "Come."

The rest of the morning passed with Boss on Ginger's lap as she added figures to the ledger. Before she knew it, Pippins tapped on the door. "Madam, Lady Davenport-Witt is here to see you."

"Oh mercy," Ginger said. "I forgot about our luncheon." Ginger carefully set Boss on the carpet and got to her feet. "Please tell her I'm on my way."

Felicia playfully honked the horn of the two-seater Mercedes-Benz, the latest addition to the Davenport-Witt collection. It was painted a soft yellow with a long, narrow bonnet, swooping black wings, and white-rimmed spoked tyres. Ginger couldn't help but smile. She and Felicia might legally no longer be sisters, but they'd rubbed off on each other. Felicia wore a remarkably similar cloche hat and spring jacket ensemble to Ginger's.

"Great minds think alike," Ginger said as she sat on the tan-leather passenger seat.

The drive to the riverside restaurant was quiet, as Felicia had made it clear she couldn't focus on driving and conversation simultaneously. Ginger prided herself on being more versatile but respected Felicia's need for quiet, though she couldn't help but silently urge her to put more weight on the accelerator. At the rate Felicia puttered along, they'd share dinner, not luncheon, together.

Felicia surprised Ginger by breaking her own no-talking rule. "Isn't that Helen Forbes?"

Ginger caught sight of Miss Forbes standing on the pavement, a placard in hand that read, "Equal voting rights for women."

"It is," Ginger said. "I have to admire her stamina."

Felicia pulled her motorcar to the kerb and brought it to a stop.

"You're lucky you're over thirty, Ginger, and with the necessary property qualifications. I'm a married woman, run a household, employ and pay my own staff, and still have no say in how things are run in my country. It's ludicrous."

Ginger couldn't agree more. "It's dreadfully unfair."

"Charles says change is coming."

"Thanks to ladies like Miss Forbes," Ginger said. "It's unfortunate that she's not more organised, with other women to support her. She's coming across as rather unhinged."

As Ginger spoke these words, Miss Forbes wielded her sign like a sword, and when Ginger realised the object of the woman's ire, Mr. Gerald Hall, she could hardly blame her. She stepped out of the motorcar and picked up her pace, hoping to intercept them before the two incited a public brawl. Felicia was on her heels.

Ginger called out, "Miss Forbes! Mr. Hall!"

Thankfully the two came to their senses when they heard their names called out. Mr. Hall's face was red with barely controlled rage. Miss Forbes' crooked smile betrayed bemusement.

"This woman is a menace!" Mr. Hall bellowed. "She should be arrested!"

"Are you threatening me, Mr. Hall?" Miss Forbes asked.

Tugging on his waistcoat, the politician put on a

practiced smile of cool collection. "I'll not let you rattle me, Miss Forbes. You and your lot can already vote at thirty, a policy I still oppose. Your behaviour is continued proof that you can't handle the responsibility." He doffed his trilby in Ginger and Felicia's direction. "Good day, ladies."

Miss Forbes laughed heartily at the man's back. "There goes a man who is most definitely rattled."

"That was quite a public display, Miss Forbes," Ginger said.

"You say that as if you disapprove, Mrs. Reed."

"I do admire your dedication to the cause, though—"

Miss Forbes' runaway brows jumped. "Though?"

"I'm wondering if your efforts would be more successful with a bit of organisation. In fact, Lady Davenport-Witt and I were just discussing how we could urge governmental change when we spotted you here."

Felicia's eyes widened at the embellishment, but she nodded. "That's right. I am also eager to vote this year, though I currently don't qualify."

Miss Forbes' thin shoulders relaxed. "It certainly would be nice to have more ladies like you rallying for change. I realise my methods have been rash and uncouth. It stems from deep anger and frustration, but I'm not stupid. I understand a change in methodology might be more acceptable."

"Lady Davenport-Witt and I were just about to have lunch," Ginger said. "Would you like to join us?"

Miss Forbes' gaze darted to the fancy restaurant, and Ginger immediately knew her error. Miss Forbes didn't have the finances for such a fine establishment, so Ginger quickly added, "Or, if you're busy, you could come to my residence for lunch. Would tomorrow suit you?"

Miss Forbes smiled back with appreciation. "Yes, tomorrow would suit me fine, thank you."

"Terrific," Ginger said. She gave Miss Forbes her Mallowan Court address. "Would one o'clock be suitable?"

"Thank you," Miss Forbes said. "I'll be there." She lowered her placard and disappeared into the crowd.

"What an interesting woman," Felicia said.

"Indeed," Ginger agreed. "Now then, let's move on. I'm famished."

THE NEXT DAY, Ginger found Haley in the library at Hartigan House, her nose in a book.

"You're home," Ginger said. "I was beginning to think you lived at the hospital."

"The dead may not sleep or study, but I still have to," Haley said without looking up. The wingback chair she was curled up in—a feat made easy because she wore trousers—faced a lit fireplace. "I have an exam coming up."

Ginger meandered across the carpeting to the window, pausing by the empty desk where Scout used to sit when he'd been tutored. Ginger missed her son, but sending children away to boarding school was a British institution, particularly amongst the upper classes. She was hardly the only mother who wrestled melancholy whilst their child was away, getting a good education.

Shelves filled with books dominated every wall. Ginger scanned the collection, her gaze eventually resting on the first edition copy of *Dracula*.

Haley's voice came from behind her. "You're making me nervous."

Ginger pulled the deep yellow hard-covered book off the shelf and ran a fingernail over the blood-red, boxy font printed near the top edge. "Remember when we got this?"

"I do. It was during the time you were busy restocking your library."

"Indeed. I find it immensely intriguing how one story can captivate a nation."

"The world, Ginger," Haley said. "Americans are also taken." She put her textbook down. "I bet Bram Stoker would be surprised."

"Why do artists and writers get the most acclaim after death?"

"Death has a certain mystique," Haley answered.

"Is that why you like working with the dead?"

"It's one of the reasons." Haley pressed a palm against her stomach. "But I remain a part of the living and need sustenance. I don't suppose Mrs. Beasley would mind rousing up a sandwich for me?"

"I'm quite certain she wouldn't," Ginger said. "In fact, Miss Forbes is about to be my guest for lunch. You should join us."

"I wouldn't want to impose."

"Nonsense. Had I known you'd be around, I would automatically have extended the invitation."

"In that case, I'd be happy to."

Ginger left Haley to wrap up her studies and descended the staircase to the kitchen to let them know that Haley would be joining her and Miss Forbes in the dining room.

At one o'clock, Ginger and Haley were in the sitting room, waiting for Miss Forbes. Once she arrived, they'd make their way to the dining room, where a luncheon prepared by the cook awaited. Coffee had been brought to the sitting room, and Ginger and Haley sipped as they chatted away the time.

"I didn't know you and Miss Forbes were friends," Haley said. "When you introduced me to her at Madame Tussaud's, it seemed you were merely acquaintances."

"We are only acquaintances and barely that," Ginger said. "But we have a common interest—we both want to carve a path for women to have a better future. Her ideas are more radical and disorganized than mine." Ginger relayed the nasty encounter she'd interrupted between Miss Forbes and Mr. Hall. "Right in the middle of the pavement."

Haley raised a brow. "So, you plan to calm her down?"

"Not in the sense that I'd want to see her zeal squelched, only more efficiently directed."

Haley flicked her wrist and frowned as she stared at her wristwatch. "Your friend is fifteen minutes late."

Ginger took a quick look at her own wristwatch, confirming the statement. "Miss Forbes might've encountered some difficulty getting here. If my

Crossley weren't in the garage, I'd have collected her myself or at least sent Clement to fetch her."

After thirty minutes, Ginger suggested that they start without Miss Forbes. "Something must've come up."

They made quick work of the lunch as they discussed the case. "I'm worried too much time is passing," Ginger said.

Haley agreed. "The more time that goes by, the less likely the murderer will be caught."

"And I'm concerned about Miss Forbes," Ginger added. "Perhaps it's in her nature to lose track of time, but I know she respects me. She'd have sent a message by now with an apology."

"Some people don't bother with tokens of courtesy."

Ginger frowned. "I don't know. Something doesn't feel right."

"Do you want to look for her?" Haley asked. "She could give you her apology in person."

"That's rather a good idea." Ginger pushed away from the table. "Though I'm not after an apology. I just want to make sure she's all right."

Digby rang for a taxicab. Thirty minutes later, the driver parked in front of a row of brick, flat-faced terraced houses. Some residences had offices at street level with flats above and bedsits in the basement.

Ginger led Haley to one of them. "This is Miss Forbes' office. My understanding is she has a bedsit downstairs."

The office door was locked. Haley cupped her eyes and stared through the window. "Doesn't look like anyone's in there."

Ginger was already heading into the stairwell next to the front door, knocking on the basement door as she called, "Miss Forbes?"

"Does she live alone?" Haley asked.

Ginger nodded. "The flat is hardly large enough for two people." This time she was the one to cup her eyes and stare through the adjacent window. She couldn't make out much, but it looked like a side table had been toppled.

"I think she's in trouble," Ginger said. After a glance over her shoulder, proving that they weren't being watched, she removed the bundle of lock picks from her handbag and went to work. Soon the lock clicked open.

"That has to be record timing," Haley said.

As expected, the bedsit comprised a single room, with a kitchenette on one end and a narrow bed, wardrobe, and a single sofa on the other. Miss

Forbes lay stretched out on her back on the sofa as if she were merely napping.

Ginger didn't bother trying to wake her. The bluish-white pallor of her skin and the two red marks on her neck told her that Helen Forbes was already dead.

18

*G*inger waved down a passing bobby and had him ring for Basil. When she returned to Helen Forbes' flat, she found Haley doing a preliminary check on the body.

"Same modus operandi as the others," Haley said as she turned to Ginger. "Though there appear to be more contusions on her arms. Possibly trace evidence under her fingernails. Her nails look cared for, so I doubt she'd purposely leave debris under them."

"She fought back," Ginger said. "And that's not the only difference between her and the others. She's not a lady of the night."

Ginger pointed this out to Basil when he and Constable Braxton arrived on the scene.

"Perhaps it's a copycat," Basil said. "Word of how the other victims have died has got out."

Haley shook her head. "A copycat wouldn't have the exact same puncture marks. I'll know more when we can properly examine the injury, but this appears to be the same dimensions, both in the spacing and the size of the marks."

Other officers arrived, and Basil carefully organised them to ensure no evidence was disturbed. A few were instructed to canvass the area to see if anyone had seen anything unusual—maybe a man had come to visit Miss Forbes?—another policeman with a camera took photographs. Constable Braxton was tasked with searching the bedsit.

"Do you mind if I have a look around as well?" Ginger asked.

Basil's lips twitched into a slight smile. "I'd expect no less."

With her gloves on, Ginger opened the drawers of Helen's chest of drawers as Constable Braxton looked on. Naturally, he was uncomfortable sweeping his fingers through a woman's underthings and was happy to let Ginger carry out the task. Miss Forbes had been a practical woman, which translated into the undergarments she chose. Nothing in the drawer suggested she had had a secret or alternate lifestyle that would take her into the streets after dark.

A further search found nothing more than a pamphlet, the same one all patrons had been given on the museum's opening day, inscribed with the title: *The New Madame Tussaud's Exhibition: Official Guide and Catalogue 1928*. It had an oval sepia photograph of Madame Tussaud herself on the cover. Ginger had the same publication sitting on her desk in her study and had immensely enjoyed perusing it. One shampoo advert in particular had stood out to her, featuring two young women with short dark hair. Ginger had pondered if she should run an advertisement for Feathers & Flair in the next edition.

"Mrs. Reed?"

Ginger turned to Constable Braxton's voice. "Yes?"

"Look at this." The constable held out a promotional poster encouraging people to vote for Gerald Hall. The politician's face was scratched out.

"Oh mercy," Ginger said. "There was certainly no love lost between them."

Showing Basil and Haley the poster, Ginger said, "Felicia and I witnessed a public row between them yesterday. Had we not arrived in time to intervene,

I'm not sure what would've happened. That encounter prompted me to invite Miss Forbes for lunch today. I'd hoped to guide her towards more productive ways of getting her—*our*—message across." To Basil, she added, "Perhaps it's time to have a chat with Mr. Hall."

"Indeed," Basil said. "We'll call at his office when we've finished here."

Dr. Palmer arrived as Constable Braxton left.

"I got here as soon as I could." Dr. Palmer removed his hat as he sat his black bag on the floor of Miss Forbes' bedsit. Ginger noted how his gaze lingered a few moments on Haley before taking in the body.

"Same means of death as the Madame Tussaud's victim," Haley said.

Dr. Palmer removed his gloves, and Ginger noticed the ring on his thumb. "Look, Basil," she said. "Even the doctor is wearing a ring." At Dr. Palmer's surprised look, she added, "I bought one for Basil for Christmas, but he refuses to wear it. I think it's nice that men are moving beyond tie clips and cufflinks."

"I wear it," Basil said with a note of defensiveness. "I just don't think it's appropriate for the Yard." Such rings had become a status symbol for prominent men, and Ginger understood that Basil didn't want to draw attention to himself in that way whilst on the job.

"I know, love," Ginger said. "I'm just teasing you."

Dr. Palmer made the same cursory exam as Haley had. "Not much more to add except what comes up from the autopsy."

"I'm curious to see if the same poison was used," Haley said. "And what we find under the fingernails."

Dr. Palmer busied himself with this bag. "Indeed. I'll accompany the body to the mortuary. I assume you'd like to join me, Miss Higgins, but don't you have an exam coming up?"

"I studied this morning, Dr. Palmer," Haley said. "I would like to join you on this post-mortem."

Ginger cast a glance at Basil as she held in a smile. These two might play it safe with each other, but Ginger knew budding love when she saw it.

"And I suppose *you'd* like to join me when I speak to Mr. Hall," Basil said knowingly. As an occasional consultant to the Yard, Ginger had certain privileges. "You must promise not to antagonise the man though."

Ginger walked with Basil out to his motorcar. "I can promise no such thing."

. . .

THE RIDE back to the mortuary was a quiet one. Haley noticed Dr. Palmer's tight grip on the steering wheel and the pinched look around his eyes. Having so many women come through the mortuary in such a short period was disconcerting, and Haley shared Dr. Palmer's disquiet.

They arrived before the body was removed from the ambulance.

"Prep the table," Dr. Palmer instructed.

"Are we starting on her right away?" Haley asked, surprised. They had another post-mortem in the cool cupboard that had come in the night before.

Dr. Palmer's face flashed briefly with annoyance, and Haley stiffened. She'd never have challenged a superior if she hadn't felt a familiarity like the one that had developed between her and Dr. Palmer.

Before she could apologise, Dr. Palmer said, "I'm certain Scotland Yard would be pleased to get whatever information we can offer as soon as possible."

"Of course," Haley said and immediately began preparations. If they did the other body, another doctor might get scheduled to do Miss Forbes' autopsy, which meant Haley might miss out on the experience. Because of her connection with Basil and Ginger, she wanted to be part of this one.

The ambulance attendants lifted the body onto the porcelain surgical table, and Dr. Palmer signed the accompanying papers. They washed their hands and donned their white aprons.

"I'm sorry for snapping," Dr. Palmer said as they approached the table.

"No need to apologise." Haley held out a palm. "I was out of order."

"Let's put it behind us," Dr. Palmer said as he picked up the scalpel. "Dinner tonight?"

He held the sharp instrument to Haley, offering her the opportunity to perform the Y incision. Surely, not as a reward for saying yes to his offer? "That would be nice."

Miss Forbes' lifeless body lay exposed on the table. Haley moved the sheet down to her waist, giving her whatever dignity she could, even in death. With a steady hand, she cut. Haley had to focus as the incision was long, although a still heart meant no profuse bleeding. Still, she was aware of Dr. Palmer in her periphery. As she worked, he cleaned the debris under Miss Forbes' fingernails, depositing the evidence in a small tube.

However, instead of immediately labelling it and

putting it aside, Haley saw him slip the vial into his pocket. To keep from mislaying it?

"Oh, let me help," he said quickly.

The blood started to thicken, and Dr. Palmer used a syringe to get samples. "My bet is on Nevomax."

Haley agreed. "I can't see why the killer would change his modus operandi now."

"Though he has changed it somewhat," Dr. Palmer said, "as Miss Forbes is the first to make her living honestly."

"That is an interesting change," Haley said. "Which makes me think a copycat killer might be at work."

Dr. Palmer sighed. "That's all we need. Two killers on the rampage."

They finished the post-mortem requirements and stored Miss Forbes' body in the cool cupboard. "I imagine her next of kin are being notified." Haley's mood darkened with memories of her brother's death—the *worst* kind of news.

Dr. Palmer seemed to read her mind. "Don't think about it, Haley. There's nothing more you can do . . ." He smiled. ". . . Except get ready for a night out. Shall I pick you up?"

Haley didn't want to deal with the family fuss if a

man came to pick her up at Hartigan House. That meeting could wait until she felt more certain about a future with Dr. Palmer. "I can meet you," she said.

"Very well," Dr. Palmer replied. "If you take a taxicab to my flat, we'll have a drink before we go. There's a lovely eatery just around the corner."

GERALD HALL NARROWED his eyes as his shoulders tensed. "I'm a very busy man," he said on seeing Basil standing in the doorway of his office. "You might make an appointment with my secretary."

"We only want to ask a few questions," Basil said. "Surely you, as a person who serves the community, would want to do what you can to help the police."

Ginger stepped out from behind Basil. Gerald Hall huffed. "*You*. I should've known."

Basil motioned for Mr. Hall to sit at his desk, then pulled out a chair in front of it for Ginger before taking the remaining one for himself. He'd learned early on that Ginger had a way of getting people to talk, especially men. "You don't mind if my wife joins us, do you? She's familiar with the case and might provide unique insight."

The man exhaled without giving an opinion either way. "Should I call my solicitor?"

"I don't think that'll be necessary," Basil said, "but the decision is yours."

Hall flicked his wrist for a glance at his wristwatch. "I don't have the time to waste. Let's just get on with this, eh?"

"You and Miss Forbes were often at loggerheads, weren't you?" Ginger said.

Hall barely held in a sneer. "What of it? Suffragettes have been the bane of existence for society for years now. It's nothing new."

"You engaged in a very public row, Mr. Hall," Ginger continued.

"As I said, women like her have been like small biting dogs to politicians for decades."

"What were you discussing?" Basil asked.

"Specifically?" Hall huffed. "I hardly remember. What is this all about anyway? Why do you care so much about Helen Forbes?"

"Miss Forbes is dead," Basil said.

Hall had the decency to show shock. "Well, that's unfortunate for her, but what on earth does it have to do with me?"

"Unfortunately, Miss Forbes' end came by foul play." Basil made a point of removing his notebook and jotting a random scribble. He hoped the ruse would encourage cooperation. "It's normal police procedure to try to map out a victim's last steps," he continued. "Mrs. Reed and her companion Lady Davenport-Witt knew of Miss Forbes' interaction with you. It's a starting point, Mr. Hall, as we're unaware of who else she went to see yesterday."

Hall blew a blast of air from his cheeks. "I don't know what to say. We had words. She stormed off. I never saw her again."

"What did you do?" Ginger started. "After we left you on the street yesterday afternoon."

"Not that I have to answer to you, Mrs. Reed, but I came back to my office to work. I had lunch at my desk. And if you must know, a nap on the sofa I have here. I worked late."

"What time did you get home?" Basil asked.

Hall blew a big loud raspberry. "You said I wasn't a suspect, but this sounds like an interrogation."

Basil raised his palms. "Merely wanting to cross you off the list, Mr. Hall."

"I shouldn't be on a list, Chief Inspector, but I'll answer to satisfy you. I got in at ten o'clock."

"Can someone verify that?" Basil asked.

Hall slammed his hands on his legs before jumping to his feet. "I refuse to answer any more questions without my solicitor present. Unless you're going to arrest me for something, Chief Inspector, I appeal to you to make your exit."

"Very well," Basil said cordially. "We bid you good day."

"I don't think he likes that I'm qualified to vote," Ginger said once she and Basil were in Basil's motorcar. "I meet both the age and property requirements."

Basil smiled. "You don't look a day over thirty."

"So kind of you to say so, love." She smiled, her green eyes sparkling the way they did. "But that man is not getting my vote."

Back at the Yard, Braxton approached with a glint of excitement in his eyes.

"What is it?" Basil asked.

"The background on Arthur Keene showed something interesting, sir. Turns out he's the half-brother of Helen Forbes. Same mother, different fathers."

Basil and Ginger shared a look. "The plot thickens," Ginger said.

"Indeed," Basil agreed. To Braxton, he said, "Bring Keene in for questioning."

19

*G*inger waited with Basil at the Yard until Arthur Keene was brought in. Constable Braxton said officers had been dispatched to Madame Tussaud's Museum, where it was presumed Mr. Keene would be working.

"Miss Forbes never mentioned a brother," Ginger said, "though we weren't especially close enough to discuss family dynamics. Very odd, though, that she and Mr. Keene were both at the museum when Miss Oakley's body was found there. One would never have guessed the two were even acquainted."

Basil shrugged. "I suppose there was no reason to disclose their estrangement before now."

"Whoever is killing these women is most definitely

a misogynist." Ginger scowled at the thought. "Besides immoral women, he must hate intelligent women who 'don't know their place'—which is why I surmise that Miss Forbes was attacked—and those he perceives as immoral, as they reflect his moral weaknesses."

"Indeed," Basil said. "A reasonable profile."

"Quite an unfortunate coincidence for Mr. Keene." Ginger stared back at Basil. "A body in the museum where he is manager, and then his own sister."

Constable Braxton returned to announce that Mr. Keene was now in an interrogation room. "This also came in the post, sir. For you."

Basil opened the envelope, read the contents, and frowned deeply.

Ginger stretched out a hand to touch his arm. "What is it?"

Basil silently handed the single piece of paper to Ginger. "I'm afraid our killer has taken to writing letters to the Yard."

Ginger locked her eyes on Basil. "Is this the first one?"

He gave a subtle shake of his head. "There've been three others. Short like this one. Morris prevented me from sharing them with anyone, but now, I think he's willing for me to do anything if it'll help me make an arrest."

Ginger focused on the note in her hand. The ink was smooth, suggesting an expensive fountain pen, and the ink choice was neither the usual blue nor black but a deep blood red.

> *Chief Inspector,*
>
> *How high can you count? Higher than five? I've only just got started.*
>
> *D*

Oh mercy. She stared back at Basil. "I wonder what 'D' stands for?"

"Dracula? I hardly think he'd use his real initial, but one can never underestimate the vanity of another," Basil said. "I'll send a man to keep an eye on Hartigan House."

Ginger nodded her agreement, but even the knowledge of a competent lawman to keep watch over her property didn't keep her stomach from clenching. The best thing they could do was catch this villain and stop him once and for all.

Following Basil, Ginger sat beside him on the opposite side of the table from Mr. Keene. Basil gave his usual instruction and reasoning for Ginger's presence. Mr. Keene looked down his nose as he glanced at Ginger with disinterest.

Basil ducked his chin. "Let me begin by expressing consolation for your loss, Mr. Keene."

"Thank you," Mr. Keene said.

"Were you and your sister close?" Ginger asked.

Mr. Keene snorted. "I'm gathering that you already know the answer, which is why I'm being treated like a criminal. No, we were not close."

"You must forgive us for prying," Basil said, "but your sister was murdered, and the means of her death is the same as the one used to kill Miss Oakley, who was found in your museum exhibition."

Fear flashed behind Mr. Keene's eyes. "I didn't know. The officers didn't say."

"Why were you and your sister estranged?" Ginger asked.

"Half-sister," Mr. Keene replied. "There are eight years between us. I'm the elder. I wasn't around when she was growing up, and our mother wasn't the, well, kindest. Helen resented me for abandoning her. I honoured her desire to stay out of touch." With a sigh of resignation, he continued, "Of course, with us both living in London, it's natural that we'd run into each other on occasion, but we never spoke unless necessary."

"Did your sister know you worked at the museum?" Basil asked.

Mr. Keene shrugged. "It wasn't a secret. My presence somewhere wouldn't keep Helen from attending. If you knew her, you'd know she was a very strong-minded woman."

"I understand that everyone deals with grief in their own way," Basil said, "but you don't seem very distraught."

Mr. Keene stared back dejectedly. "One can't mourn something one has never had, Chief Inspector."

"To your knowledge, did Helen have a connection with Dinah Oakley, or any of the other victims, including Annie Camden?" Ginger asked.

Shaking his head, Mr. Keene said, "No. I didn't know my sister well, but I did know her views on the lifestyles of such women. She felt they were demeaning themselves."

Basil raised a brow. "What are your views on such women?"

Mr. Keene squinted. "I don't know what you mean."

"More to the point, then," Basil started, "did you visit the Swan House on occasion?"

"I most certainly did not!"

"We have a witness who says otherwise," Basil said.

Mr. Keene blanched. "A witness? That's not possible."

Basil remained silent.

"Who?" Mr. Keene demanded,

"I'm afraid I can't disclose that," Basil said.

"How can I defend myself if I don't know my accuser?"

"Very well," Basil said with a sigh. "It was Mr. Lockhart."

Mr. Keene blinked back with a look of disbelief. "Kenneth? That doesn't make sense."

"Why not?" Basil pressed.

Mr. Keene stared at his hands as if deliberating and coming to a conclusion. "Might I speak to Mrs. Reed alone?" He stared back at Basil.

Ginger and Basil shared a look of surprise at the request. Ginger nodded her assent.

Basil tugged on his trousers as he stood. "Very well. But understand, Mr. Keene, I'll be standing right outside the door."

"I intend Mrs. Reed no harm," Mr. Keene said.

Basil motioned to the door with his head, and Constable Braxton followed him.

When the door closed, Ginger began, "What do you want to discuss with me, Mr. Keene?"

"I perceive that you are a reasonable lady with modern views . . . perhaps more accepting of those who are . . . different from others."

Ginger had already guessed what the museum manager was hinting at. She leaned in and said softly, "You aren't the sort that enjoys the intimate company of the female sex, are you?"

"That's not strictly true," Mr. Keene said. "I rather enjoy both, something that Mr. Lockhart couldn't understand, and which angered him terribly." He sighed. "Either way, it's not a safe declaration to make, and I'm not suited for prison, no matter the reason I might be sent there."

"I completely understand, and your secret is safe with me. I'll only divulge it if necessary, but to my husband, who sides with me on this issue and will be your best advocate."

"Thank you, madam."

"Can I assume that you and Mr. Lockhart are . . . were . . . ?"

"Were, madam." Mr. Keene's fight seemed to leak out of him. "We had a terrible row."

"Do you think that's why he spoke against you, saying you visited the Swan House? Out of spite?"

Mr. Keene glanced up with glossy eyes dark with hurt. "I wouldn't have guessed it, but it appears so." He rested his palms on the table, and Ginger got a good look at his ring for the first time. She'd seen one like it recently, on the thumb of Dr. Palmer.

"That's an interesting piece of jewellery," she said. "I've only seen one other like it."

"Have you, indeed?" Mr. Keene said. "It's a novelty ring, actually, a gift—"

"From Mr. Lockhart?" Ginger prompted.

"Yes."

"Where did he get it from?"

"Just some shop in London. Seeing the line of work we're both in, he thought I'd find the story behind it amusing."

"Oh?" Ginger said. "What story is that?"

"A ring much like this once belonged to Thomas Griffiths Wainewright. He was an English artist, author, and . . ." He locked his brown-eyed gaze on Ginger. ". . . A mass murderer."

Ginger leaned back cautiously. "I've heard of Mr. Wainewright."

It was rumoured that Thomas Wainewright had Mr. Keene's lifestyle in common. Did Mr. Keene also have Wainewright's history of multiple killings in common?

Mr. Keene played with his ring. "It's been said that Mr. Wainewright owned a ring like this one, which had a special compartment to carry strychnine." He pressed the top of the ring, and it sprung open, revealing a single prong. "My ring is empty, naturally." He slipped it off and pushed it across the table. "You can have your people test it to confirm if you like."

Ginger was certain the police would thoroughly test it, but that wasn't what was bothering her now. Mr. Keene's ring had one prong. If one were to open the ring on Dr. Palmer's hand, would there be two?

20

Startling Mr. Keene, Ginger sprung out of her chair and out of the room, where she found Basil waiting in the corridor.

"Ginger?" Basil stared back with apprehension. "Are you all right?"

"Yes, I'm fine." Ginger waved her fingers, brushing Basil's concerns away. "But Mr. Keene is either innocent or an excellent storyteller. Did you notice his ring?"

Basil's lips twitched. "You seem to have developed a fascination with men's jewellery lately, particularly rings."

"Well, in this case, it's rather curious. He has a ring much the same as Dr. Palmer's. It's a novelty ring." Ginger told him about its peculiar function and the myth that Mr. Wainewright had used it to poison his victims.

Basil frowned. "I'm familiar with the case. How well do you know Dr. Neville Palmer?"

"About as well as you do," Ginger said. "He came to London two months ago and has stepped in for Dr. Gupta on this case. He seems to fancy Haley . . ." Ginger's heart skipped. "But, no, Haley doesn't meet the profile."

"Not of the Swan House women, but she's rather a lot like Miss Forbes," Basil said soberly. "Educated, intelligent, driven to succeed in her vocation where men dominate." To Constable Braxton, he said, "Let Mr. Keene go but warn him to stay in London. I'm taking Mrs. Reed to visit the University College Hospital mortuary."

Ginger's anxiety grew as Basil drove his Austin to the hospital. She tried to shake off her sense of apprehension. Dr. Palmer was courteous and gracious, taking medicine and the Hippocratic oath seriously. Ginger was letting this case get under her skin. Certainly, he had said things in jest that could be taken as a slight towards the finer sex, but that was common with many men and didn't make them killers—*no need to put grotesque images into your lovely head, Mrs. Reed.*

Ginger was sure that once they spoke to Dr. Palmer and examined his ring—she would come up with some ruse of being enthralled by the piece to entice him to hand it over to her—she'd see her nerves were for nothing and would laugh it off.

As if sensing Ginger's trepidation, Basil reached for her hand and said, "We'll just drop in and see if anything new has come from Miss Forbes' post-mortem. I would be interested in knowing if she died of the same poison as the others."

"Haley could be trying to reach us now," Ginger said. "If only one could carry a telephone device on one's person, to be reached at any time." She stared at Basil wide-eyed. "Can you imagine it?"

Basil chortled. "That would be ghastly. One would never get a moment's peace."

THE MORTUARY at the University College Hospital was eerily quiet. Only the caretaker was there to let them inside, with Basil's encouragement. Ginger knew where the light switch was located, and the light brightened the area around the desks and storage shelves.

"Is it all right for us to snoop around?" Ginger asked.

Basil chuckled. "Since when have rules around snooping ever stopped you?"

"Since my dear friend Haley is involved and could object."

"She won't object," Basil said. "We're here on police business. It's just unfortunate that neither she nor Palmer is here."

"Perhaps there's a file on Miss Forbes that will tell us about the poison," Ginger said. She opened the top file of the standing cabinet between the desk Haley used as an intern and Dr. Palmer's small office. A glance inside his room proved no filing cabinets were there. All the files were kept in the cabinets in the larger, open area. Finding the files for the initial "F", Ginger pulled a file for "Forbes, Helen" near the front and fished through it. "These are copies," she said. Scanning the document, she found the word "Nevomax". "It's the same poison," she announced. "Nevomax is the killer's poison of choice." After reading the rest of the report, Ginger frowned. "I remember Haley pointing out that Helen had fought back, and there was visible skin tissue under her nails, but there's nothing written here. Wait, oh, Haley made a note that the results were inconclusive."

Basil, who'd opened the drawer of a second tall

cabinet, grunted. "There's a file for a man called Palmer," he said. "A relation?"

Ginger stepped to Basil's side and read over his shoulder. "William Palmer. Died in 1856 by hanging. Here's a newspaper clipping."

Basil picked up the clipping and read aloud. "William Palmer, also called Palmer the Poisoner, was convicted in 1855 for the murder of his friend John Cook whom he'd poisoned with strychnine." He stared up at Ginger before continuing. "He was suspected of poisoning several other people, including his brother- and mother-in-law, as well as four of his own children."

Ginger's hand went to her throat. "Oh mercy."

Basil referred back to the file. "There's nothing else here."

"Why would that file be in there?" Ginger asked. "Are there any other similar files? Try Thomas Griffiths Wainewright."

Basil's fingers moved quickly. "Wainewright," he said. Looking closely, he pinched his lips. "It's the murderer." He named several other famous British mass murderers. "Jack the Ripper is the most obvious. Also included are the likes of Mary Ann Cotton, Amelia Dyer, and the duo Burke and Hare."

"Here is a file for Jack the Ripper," Ginger said. A

quick search produced the others. "There are hundreds of files," she added. "Haley hadn't yet made the connection."

"An interest in mass murderers isn't evidence of a crime," Basil said. "And many might say it's natural for a pathologist to follow such notorious killings and deaths. If Palmer is our man, we need something else."

Ginger and Basil began to open the drawers, searching even the ones that contained bodies. Ginger opened one drawer and, finding no evidence, closed it to open another until she finally came across the one bearing Miss Forbes.

"Oh, Helen," she said softly. "You certainly didn't deserve this."

"Ginger?"

Turning towards Basil's voice, she responded when he waved her over to the desk used by the doctors. Basil held a sheet of paper in his hand, his eyes pinching as he stared intensely.

"What is it?" Ginger asked.

Basil handed the paper to Ginger. She perused it and then looked up at her husband. "It looks like a standard form."

"It's the handwriting." He pulled out the latest note he'd received from the killer. "Our man uses the same type of pen; look, the ink is the same shade of red."

The handwriting was clearly from the same hand. Ginger's heart grew cold as her eyes moved to the signature at the bottom of the form. *Dr. Neville Palmer.*

21

*H*aley batted back a thread of nervousness. It was a sensation she didn't normally struggle with, but Dr. Palmer affected her in ways she hadn't felt before. Not that she hadn't been on dates, but this one felt different for some reason. She was even wearing a touch of lipstick. Haley didn't own a bit of make-up, but Ginger had offered hers several times. Lizzie helped her access it—Haley knew Ginger wouldn't mind.

Exiting the taxicab in front of the address Dr. Palmer had given her, Haley took a moment to inhale deeply before heading inside the four-storey residential building. Haley rarely visited a gentleman's flat unaccompanied, but Dr. Palmer was different. He was a trusted physician and a respectable citizen of the city of London. Sure, he could be cavalier about certain matters, but when working with the dead, it helped to have a sense of humour, even if it lent itself to irony or sarcasm.

Catching her reflection in the mirror, Haley paused to smooth out the crepe satin of her navy-blue, long-sleeved dress. Her ensemble was much more subdued than what she'd worn to the Italian restaurant and, quite frankly, much more in keeping with her laid-back style. Lizzie had offered to style her hair into a faux bob and had done a much neater job than Haley could ever do alone. Her curls had remained obedient under Lizzie's skilful hands, and only one small one strayed onto her forehead. She carefully tucked it behind her ears, then stepped into the cage lift.

The attendant doffed his uniform hat. "Which floor, madam?"

"Third, please."

After closing the door, the attendant flicked a switch, and the elevator began its ascent. "Are we off to visit Dr. Palmer?"

"Yes." Haley blinked back her surprise. Surely Dr. Palmer wasn't the only tenant on the third floor? Why would the attendant assume that? "Does Dr. Palmer have a lot of visitors?"

The attendant pressed the buttons on their arrival and opened the cage doors. "Oh, that's not for me to say, madam."

Haley entered the hallway and found the doctor's apartment at the end by the stairs. After taking a calming breath and patting curls into place, she knocked.

Dr. Palmer opened the door to her with a welcoming smile. His apartment was sparsely decorated and lacked any feminine touches. The simple, though quality, furniture seemed too small for the space. The fireplace was lit and cast a warm and inviting glow. Dr. Palmer's complexion, normally pale under the harsh lights in the mortuary, had an attractive flush, likely resulting from the effects of the amber drink in the crystal glass he held in his hand.

"Come in, Haley," he said. "I'm having a little pre-dinner drink. Would you like one?"

"Sure," she said. "Thank you."

As Dr. Palmer poured from the decanter on the sideboard, Haley fought back her nervousness by perusing the bookshelf. Seeing what kinds of books people bought and saved was always interesting, and Dr. Palmer's collection was intriguing. There even a book penned by Gerald Hall, *Under the*

Carpet. Haley had perused it during a visit to Hatchards. It was a manifesto on the wickedness of modern society and radical ways to bring change. It would help to stop sweeping Britain's problems under the proverbial rug—a carpet in British parlance.

Hidden between a dictionary and an atlas was a copy of *Mein Kampf*. An intriguing addition to a personal library, but well-read types wanted to be abreast of all types of philosophy. A copy of *Dracula* was propped up face out. Haley thumbed through it. The pages were dog-eared, and the volume had been well read. She held it up. "I see you're a fan of Bram Stoker as well."

"Certainly." He handed Haley's drink to her as she set the book down. "I've been to Scotland to visit the castle which inspired the book."

"Oh? Lord and Lady Davenport-Witt have just returned from there. Felicia had expected something bigger and eerier."

"Clearly, she didn't visit after dark." Dr. Palmer sipped his drink, then continued. "It's the lore that's fascinating. And the concept of drinking blood from a beautiful maiden's neck. It's tantalising, isn't it?"

Tantalising wasn't the word that came to Haley. More like a gruesome fetish.

"I don't like romanticising violence," Haley said, trying to keep her voice light.

"Of course not," Dr. Palmer said. "I'm speaking in a literary sense. One must separate fact from fiction. Men are men, and women are women."

Haley stiffened. "What do you mean by that?"

"Only that modern times have confused people about their place in society." Dr. Palmer set his empty glass down. "Women wanting the vote, taking jobs from family men, things like that."

"Like *me*?" Haley said incredulously. "I've cast a vote in America. I'm working in a male-dominated field."

Dr. Palmer chortled. "I'm jesting, Miss Higgins. It's your rebellious nature that I find so exciting." He ran a finger around his collar, loosening the top button. "I'm finding it rather warm in here," he said. "Do you think it's warm?" He rolled up his sleeves as he stepped closer.

Blood rushed to Haley's head as she took in the scratch marks on Dr. Palmer's arms, most certainly caused by fingernails.

Her mind flashed to the moment in the mortuary during Miss Forbes' post-mortem, when she'd glimpsed Dr. Palmer slipping a vial with the evidence gathered from under the woman's fingernails into his pocket and how the test results for them never came back with the rest of the report.

Her eyes darted to Dr. Palmer's, his glossing over with deepening darkness. She knew, and he knew that she knew.

Dr. Palmer ran his neatly manicured fingers over the fist of his right hand. His eyes deadened. "Let me tell you about my ring."

Haley struggled to swallow. It was as if the Dr. Palmer she knew, the Dr. Palmer she thought she knew, slipped away behind a monster encased by the same skin—Dr. Neville Palmer's own Jekyll and Hyde.

Haley took a careful step backwards, the heat from the embers in the fireplace warming her back. "It's a lovely ring," she said carefully.

Dr. Palmer chuckled. "It's not just a ring, Haley. It's a mechanism for death." He pressed the top, and it snapped open, revealing two prongs inside.

"That is how you did it?" Haley said, pushing through blackening fear.

"Indeed. The ring has a compartment where you can inject poison."

"You press the prongs against your unwitting victims," Haley said with bitter understanding dawning, "destining them to a slow, painful death."

"I keep them comfortable in my bed," Dr. Palmer said harshly. "I'm not a monster."

"But you are, Dr. Palmer," Haley said, forcing her voice to remain steady. "You are the very definition of a monster. And worse, you're deceptive, not giving your victims a chance to fight back."

"Not all, perhaps," Dr. Palmer said. "The ones prior to Miss Forbes were very compliant, removing their clothing and slipping under my covers without question. They didn't see what was coming, so in that regard, I showed kindness. And I contributed to the good of society by removing immoral temptresses from London's streets."

Haley could hardly believe her ears. Dr. Palmer's twisted sense of justice and what it meant to be kind. How had she missed this?

"Why Miss Forbes, then?" Haley asked, wanting to keep Dr. Palmer talking. Rapidly assessing her situation, she broke out in a cold sweat as she concluded that her predicament was dire. Dr. Palmer blocked the route to the door. She had no weapon, not even her glass which she'd foolishly set down out of arm's reach. If she took another step back, she'd fall into the fire.

"Miss Forbes was becoming an embarrassing nuisance. Undermining a good man like Gerald

Hall, and her relentless nattering about women wanting the vote, as if a woman could ever be man's equal."

Haley gasped at Dr. Palmer's unfiltered misogynistic outburst.

"Why did you place Miss Oakley in the Dracula exhibition?" she asked. "You weren't so theatrical with the others."

"Because you told me you and Mrs. Reed were going to attend." Dr. Palmer's lips moved upwards crookedly. "I wanted to see if you'd notice." Shaking his head, he clucked his tongue as if he disapproved. "I should've known you would."

"But how did you get her body in without anyone noticing?"

"I walked her in, naturally." Dr. Palmer smiled darkly. "When I suggested we sneak into the exhibit before it opened, she was giddy to do it. There was a lot of activity at the back entrance, people working late to get things done. I simply dressed in a pair of overalls and escorted her in." His grin deepened. "Miss Oakley loved to play the part."

A drapery of drowsiness began to settle on Haley's mind and body. Her gaze moved to her unfinished drink.

"I thought you liked me," she finally said.

Dr. Palmer smiled dryly. "I do fancy you. But you're too intelligent. You don't know your place."

"If you consider me intelligent," Haley started, "why would you condemn me to a life where I'm unable to use my mind."

"Because women like you unbalance nature, Haley." Dr. Palmer ran his hand through his hair, exasperated. "Surely you must see this. All species have a reason and purpose. Men have one, and women have another. It's just not right that you are doing what you're doing. You must be stopped."

Through Dr. Palmer's rant, Haley reached behind her back and managed to grasp the poker.

"It's not worth fighting me," Dr. Palmer said. "You're probably feeling as if you're walking through treacle by now."

"Molasses." Haley could hear her voice slurring. "That's what it's called in America."

Haley didn't know if she had dreamed it, but suddenly the blurry forms of Basil and Ginger burst into the room. Ginger's voice came to her in a thunder roll. "*Sttooppp.*"

With one last effort, Haley swung the poker like a baseball bat, catching a distracted Dr. Palmer on the side of the head, then watched as he dropped to the floor.

The next thing she knew, she woke up on Dr. Palmer's sofa, with Ginger stroking her hair. "You're going to be all right, love," Ginger said. "It was only sleeping powder."

"Dr. Palmer?" Haley croaked out.

"He's being detained," Ginger said, "but you gave him a good headache."

Haley smiled.

22

*D*r. Neville Palmer was charged with the murders of six London women, including Miss Helen Forbes, Annie Camden, and Dinah Oakley. Further investigations also linked the deaths of at least two women from Rugeley, where Dr. Palmer had resided before moving to London. It seemed he saw himself as a type of Dracula, so he signed his notes with the letter D. Perhaps he had been inspired by the fictional character, as well as the real one who also bore his surname, William Palmer. In time, Neville Palmer would be tried, convicted, and hanged for his crimes.

Ginger worried about Haley, who'd become blue for several weeks after the doctor's arrest. At least Haley hadn't fallen in love with Dr. Palmer. She was more disappointed in herself for missing the signs and being led astray by "romantic notions".

A good protest was exactly what her friend needed. The blusterous Gerald Hall was spouting off in Trafalgar Square again, and Ginger had rallied Haley and Felicia to demonstrate with her and the other suffragettes who'd come out to make their voices heard.

"It's just simply time for all British women to be given the vote, at the same age as their male counterparts and without added restrictions," Ginger said.

Haley and Felicia naturally agreed, with Haley stating, "American women have enjoyed this opportunity for eight years now."

Felicia added, "It's an embarrassment to the British government and the Crown." The three stood boldly in the square, raising placards that read: Votes for all Women Now.

Not everyone of the female persuasion agreed. Ambrosia and Mrs. Schofield scowled back at them from the other side of the street. Even if she disagreed with their politics, Ginger had to admire their gumption at such a late stage in life. Ambrosia found most things about the modernity of the twentieth century challenging to accept. However, though Ginger and the family matriarch found themselves on opposite sides of this matter, at home, they were family and remained a united front.

"I do believe the tide is turning," Felicia said. "Charles says the majority in the House of Lords are bending towards equality for women, or at least, some equality."

"I do hope he's right," Ginger returned. "Wouldn't it be nice if you could vote in the next election?"

Felicia's face brightened. "A year from now? That would be fabulous."

"It makes me feel like it's my duty to return home in time for the next American federal election," Haley said. "It's this November."

Ginger linked her arm with Haley's. "That's months away. I can't bear the thought of you leaving again."

Haley offered a sad smile. "You know I must, Ginger."

Ginger didn't like the faraway look in Haley's eyes, as if her mind was elsewhere, probably Boston, despite the current chaotic environment.

More raucous name-calling came from the other side of the square, drawing Ginger's gaze back to Ambrosia and Mrs. Schofield. Both ladies looked washed out with fatigue, and Ginger didn't like how Ambrosia was leaning heavily on her walking stick.

"I think it's time to take our opponents home before they topple over and make a scene," Ginger said. Happily, her Crossley was back on the road, running as good as new.

Felicia nodded. "Grandmama wouldn't live down the embarrassment should such a thing happen."

"Why don't you four go along," Haley said. "I'll take a taxicab."

"Nonsense," Ginger said. "The five of us can squeeze in. We'll be home in a jiffy."

Ginger saw a look of trepidation pass between Haley and Felicia, but they'd already taken strides towards the elderly ladies, stopping them from protesting further.

Despite hitting that one pothole, Ginger thought they returned to Hartigan House quite safely. Lizzie set up a tea tray for them in the sitting room, and Ginger felt contented sitting with Haley over a cup of tea and cucumber sandwiches. A cheerful fire in the hearth drove off the persistent chill that permeated the stone walls. Haley stared blankly ahead, towards the flames, her eyes seemingly locked on *The Mermaid*, a Waterhouse painting of a beautiful, red-headed creature of the sea.

Haley turned to Ginger, her wide mouth forming a sad smile. "My time in Europe has been eventful, and I've loved spending this time with you, honey."

"But . . ." Ginger prompted.

"But this isn't my home, and I've got unfinished business back in Boston."

"Joe," Ginger said gently. Joseph Higgins' death was a dark cloud that followed Haley around despite her valiant efforts to push it aside for the sake of others in the room, but Ginger sensed it often. "You may never know the truth."

"I know," Haley acknowledged. "But it's too soon to give up."

Ginger exhaled long and slow. "I hate to see you go, love, but I understand. When will you be leaving?"

"Next week. I sent a telegram to my professor at Boston University and heard back yesterday. I can complete my internship studies there."

"That's very accommodating of them," Ginger said.

Haley smirked. "Having been an intern under the skilful eye of a mass murderer has its perks."

The door opened, and Felicia and Ambrosia stepped inside. "Thank you for inviting me to join you,"

Felicia said as she assisted Ambrosia to one of the armchairs. "My house can feel large and empty without Charles around. I don't understand why he must work so much, but…" She threw up an arm. "…Such is life."

Ginger couldn't soothe Felicia's anxiety over Charles' business as she didn't know the answer herself. Sitting in the House of Lords as a member had its obligations, but Ginger suspected Charles was occupied with much more than that. Sometimes, Ginger missed the excitement of secret service work, but she only had to snuggle with Rosa or ride horses with Scout to get over the pull.

Ambrosia perked up after a cup of tea and a bite to eat.

"I'm too old for those sorts of outings," she muttered. "I don't know why I let Mrs. Schofield talk me into such things."

"I presume she's relieved that Alfred's name has been cleared," Ginger said. Alfred had moved back in with his grandmother but remained reclusive. Ginger hoped he'd get the help he needed to recover from his ailments.

"Relieved?" Ambrosia blustered. "She's irate that his name was dragged through the mud in the first place, and I don't blame her."

"That explains the cold shoulder she gave us all in the motorcar," Felicia said.

"I thought it was because she was made to sit in the middle of the backseat," Haley said. "I would've taken it gladly if not for these long legs."

"Oh, Ginger, I meant to show this to you." Fishing through her handbag, Felicia produced an unsealed envelope. "It came in this morning's post. At first, I thought it was a joke, but it was clearly addressed to me. I can hardly make any sense of it all."

Ginger accepted the envelope and removed the single, folded piece of paper from the inside. Her eyes scanned the script, the words making her stomach clench. Her gaze shot to Ambrosia across the room. The dowager Lady Gold had a secret she'd kept safely hidden for decades. The writer of this letter intended to change all that.

Dearest Lady Davenport-Witt,

Your name was GOLDen, but was that its real WORTH?

The truth is stranger than fiction. Do you really want to know it?

I do.

"Ginger?" Felicia pressed.

Ginger forced a smile. "It's nothing. It's natural for ladies in popular society to be targets of charlatans and gossipers. I wouldn't worry about it."

Felicia seemed satisfied with Ginger's response and changed the subject to photography, her new passion. Ginger responded mechanically, but she only paid attention with half her mind. The other half was on the note she'd slipped out of sight. The note and that damning diary belonging to Ambrosia, the dowager Lady Gold.

ABOUT NEVOMAX

I'm thankful to Agatha Christie for making it totally okay to invent a poison! Nevomax isn't real, but I hope you enjoy this fictional account.

UK SERIAL KILLERS IN HISTORY

Murder at Madame Tussauds is a mystery about a fictional serial killer, though there have been plenty of notorious ones in real life. I touched on a few, but the following were of particular interest to me and were referred to in more detail.

William Palmer, AKA "Palmer the Poisoner," was a doctor suspected of numerous murders, although he was only convicted of one.

He was hanged on June 14, 1856.

William Palmer (6 August 1824 – 14 June 1856), also known as the Rugeley Poisoner or the Prince of Poisoners, was an English doctor found guilty of murder in one of the most notorious cases of the 19th century. Charles Dickens called Palmer "the greatest villain that ever stood in the Old Bailey". Palmer was convicted for the 1855 murder of his friend John Cook, and was executed in public by hanging the following year. He had poisoned Cook with strychnine, and was suspected of poisoning several other people including his brother and his mother-in-law, as well as four of his children who died of "convulsions" before their first birthdays. Palmer made large sums of money from the deaths of his wife and brother after collecting on life insurance, and by defrauding his wealthy mother out of thousands of pounds, all of which he lost through gambling on horses.

Age: Deceased at 31 (1824-1856)

Birthplace: Rugeley, United Kingdom

Thomas Griffiths Wainewright was an artist who is believed to have poisoned four people.

Thomas Griffiths Wainewright (October 1794 – 17 August 1847) was an English artist, author and suspected serial killer. He gained a reputation as profligate and a dandy, and in 1837, was transported to the penal colony of Van Diemen's Land (now the Australian state of Tasmania) for frauds on the Bank of England. As a convict he became a portraitist for Hobart's elite. Wainewright's life captured the imagination of renowned 19th-century literary figures such as Charles Dickens, Oscar Wilde and Edward Bulwer-Lytton, some of whom wildly exaggerated his supposed crimes, claiming among other things that he carried strychnine in a special compartment in a ring on his finger.

Age: Dec. at 52 (1794-1847)

Birthplace: Chiswick, London, England

FOLLOW HALEY BACK TO BOSTON

Ginger visits her friend in 1932!

DEATH ON TREMONT ROW

A Higgins & Hawke Mystery #5

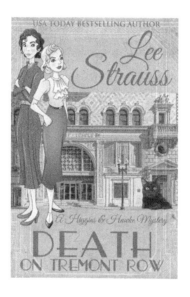

Death is greatly depressing!

It's been five years since Haley Higgins she moved back from London to Boston, and in that time she'd become a doctor of pathology and the assistant pathologist at the Boston City Morgue. In her position she often assists in the solving of crimes and murders, particularly since she's been working in tandem with Samantha Hawke, an intrepid newspaper reporter and good friend.

In the spring of 1932, depression is widespread in all its forms. Haley is cheered by news that her good friend Ginger Reed, also known as Lady Gold and a former resident of Boston, is coming to visit! Naturally, Ginger will want to spend time with her sister and stepmother, but there will certainly be time for two old friends to chum around.

Tremont Row, a bustling shopping and theatre district, is exactly the kind of place Haley and Ginger, along with Samantha, love to hang out. Until a stabbing death interferes with their shopping plans!

Haley and Samantha, continuing to fight the patriarchal barriers in their respective fields, work together to find justice for the latest victim. Is it a crime driven by the desperation of poverty, or is the motive far more sinister?

Get on AMAZON or read Free with Kindle Unlimited!

Don't miss the next Ginger Gold mystery~
MURDER AT ST. PAUL'S CATHEDRAL

Buy on AMAZON or read Free with Kindle
Unlimited!

Family secrets are murder!

When Ginger's former sister-in-law Felicia, now
Lady Davenport-Witt, first received a mysterious
note in the post, she dismissed it as coming from a
nuisance writer. These things were known to
happen to those who enjoyed social popularity. But
with a third one, she began to feel ill at ease.

Ginger, however, had been worried since the first short missive had arrived. Someone knew of a family secret that would upset Felicia's apple cart in a very big way.

Felicia's new hobby of photography turned into freelance work for a London paper, and her first assignment was to attend the wedding of the new Duke of Worthington and his very young bride-to-be taking place at St. Paul's Cathedral. Murder follows matrimony, and Felicia finds herself in the middle of the muddle.

Can Ginger help Felicia navigate the twists and turns of fate and stop a second death?

Buy on AMAZON or read Free with Kindle Unlimited!

ABOUT THE AUTHOR

Lee Strauss is a USA TODAY bestselling author of The Ginger Gold Mysteries series, The Higgins & Hawke Mystery series, The Rosa Reed Mystery series (cozy historical mysteries), A Nursery Rhyme Mystery series (mystery suspense), The Light & Love series (sweet romance), The Clockwise Collection (YA time travel romance), and young adult historical fiction with over a million books read. She has titles published in German and French, and a growing audio library.

When Lee's not writing or reading she likes to cycle, hike, and stare at the ocean. She loves to drink caffè lattes and red wines in exotic places, and eat dark chocolate anywhere.

For more info on books by Lee Strauss and her social media links, visit leestraussbooks.com. To make sure you don't miss the next new release, be sure to sign up for her readers' list!

Discuss the books, ask questions, share your

opinions. Fun giveaways! Join the Lee Strauss
Readers' Group on Facebook for more info.

Did you know you can follow your favourite authors
on Bookbub? If you subscribe to Bookbub — (and if
you don't, why don't you? - They'll send you daily
emails alerting you to sales and new releases on just
the kind of books you like to read!) — follow me to
make sure you don't miss the next Ginger Gold
Mystery!

www.leestraussbooks.com
leestraussbooks@gmail.com

MORE FROM LEE STRAUSS

On AMAZON

GINGER GOLD MYSTERY SERIES (cozy 1920s historical)

Cozy. Charming. Filled with Bright Young Things. This Jazz Age murder mystery will entertain and delight you with its 1920s flair and pizzazz!

Murder on the SS Rosa

Murder at Hartigan House

Murder at Bray Manor

Murder at Feathers & Flair

Murder at the Mortuary

Murder at Kensington Gardens

Murder at St. George's Church

The Wedding of Ginger & Basil

Murder Aboard the Flying Scotsman

Murder at the Boat Club

Murder on Eaton Square

LADY GOLD INVESTIGATES (Ginger Gold companion short stories)

HIGGINS & HAWKE MYSTERY SERIES (cozy 1930s historical)

The 1930s meets Rizzoli & Isles in this friendship depression era cozy mystery series.

Death at the Tavern

Death on the Tower

Death on Hanover

Death by Dancing

Death on Tremont Row

THE ROSA REED MYSTERIES

(1950s cozy historical)

Murder at High Tide

Murder on the Boardwalk

Murder at the Bomb Shelter

Murder on Location

Murder and Rock 'n Roll

Murder at the Races

Murder at the Dude Ranch

Murder in London

Murder at the Fiesta

Murder at the Weddings

A NURSERY RHYME MYSTERY
SERIES(mystery/sci fi)

Marlow finds himself teamed up with intelligent and savvy Sage Farrell, a girl so far out of his league he feels blinded in her presence - literally - damned glasses! Together they work to find the identity of @gingerbreadman. Can they stop the killer before he strikes again?

Gingerbread Man

Life Is but a Dream

Hickory Dickory Dock

Twinkle Little Star

LIGHT & LOVE (sweet romance)

Set in the dazzling charm of Europe, follow Katja, Gabriella, Eva, Anna and Belle as they find strength, hope and love.

Love Song

Your Love is Sweet

In Light of Us

Lying in Starlight

PLAYING WITH MATCHES (WW2 history/romance)

A sobering but hopeful journey about how one young German boy copes with the war and propaganda. Based on true events.

A Piece of Blue String (companion short story)

THE CLOCKWISE COLLECTION (YA time travel romance)

Casey Donovan has issues: hair, height and uncontrollable trips to the 19th century! And now this ~ she's accidentally taken Nate Mackenzie, the cutest boy in the school, back in time. Awkward.

Clockwise

Clockwiser

Like Clockwork

Counter Clockwise

Clockwork Crazy

Clocked (companion novella)

Standalones

Seaweed

Love, Tink

Made in the USA
Las Vegas, NV
15 October 2024